I0692759

NEWS OF
PAUL TEMPLE

Francis Durbridge

WILLIAMS & WHITING

Copyright © Serial Productions

This edition published in 2023 by Williams & Whiting

All rights reserved

This script is fully protected under the copyright laws of the
British Commonwealth of Nations, the United States of
America, and all countries of the Berne and Universal
Copyright Convention. All rights including Stage, Motion
Picture, Radio, Television, Public Reading and the right to
translate into foreign languages are strictly reserved. No part
of this publication may be lawfully reproduced in any form
or by any means such as photocopying, typescript,
manuscript, audio or video recording or digitally or
electronically or be transmitted or stored in a retrieval
system without the prior written permission of the copyright
owners.

Applications for performance or other rights should be made
to The Agency, 24 Pottery Lane, London W11 4LZ.

Cover design by Timo Schroeder

9781915887122

Williams & Whiting (Publishers)

15 Chestnut Grove, Hurstpierpoint,

West Sussex, BN6 9SS

Titles by Francis Durbridge published by Williams & Whiting

1   The Scarf – tv serial
2   Paul Temple and the Curzon Case – radio serial
3   La Boutique – radio serial
4   The Broken Horseshoe – tv serial
5   Three Plays for Radio Volume 1
6   Send for Paul Temple – radio serial
7   A Time of Day – tv serial
8   Death Comes to The Hibiscus – stage play
     The Essential Heart – radio play
     (writing as Nicholas Vane)
9   Send for Paul Temple – stage play
10   The Teckman Biography – tv serial
11   Paul Temple and Steve – radio serial
12   Twenty Minutes From Rome – a teleplay
13   Portrait of Alison – tv serial
14   Paul Temple: Two Plays for Radio Volume 1
15   Three Plays for Radio Volume 2
16   The Other Man – tv serial
17   Paul Temple and the Spencer Affair – radio serial
18   Step In The Dark – film script
19   My Friend Charles – tv serial
20   A Case For Paul Temple – radio serial
21   Murder In The Media – more rediscovered serials and
     stories
22   The Desperate People – tv serial
23   Paul Temple: Two Plays for Television
24   And Anthony Sherwood Laughed – radio series
25   The World of Tim Frazer – tv serial
26   Paul Temple Intervenes – radio serial
27   Passport To Danger! – radio serial
28   Bat Out of Hell – tv serial
29   Send For Paul Temple Again – radio serial
30   Mr Hartington Died Tomorrow – radio serial

Murder At The Weekend – the rediscovered newspaper serials and short stories

Also published by Williams & Whiting:
Francis Durbridge: The Complete Guide
By Melvyn Barnes

Titles by Francis Durbridge to be published by Williams & Whiting

Murder On The Continent (Further re-discovered serials and stories)

Operation Diplomat

Paul Temple and the Alex Affair

Paul Temple and the Canterbury Case (film script)

Paul Temple and the Conrad Case

Paul Temple and the Geneva Mystery

Paul Temple and the Margo Mystery

Paul Temple: Two Plays For Radio Vol 2 (Send For Paul Temple and News of Paul Temple)

The Passenger

INTRODUCTION

Francis Durbridge (1912-98) began his career in 1933 as a prolific writer of sketches, stories and plays for BBC radio. They were mostly light entertainments, including libretti for musical comedies, but a talent for crime fiction became evident in his early radio plays *Murder in the Midlands* (1934) and *Murder in the Embassy* (1937). The *Radio Times* (11 February 1938) mentioned that Durbridge had by then written some one hundred radio pieces, and Charles Hatton commented in *Radio Pictorial* (28 October 1938) that "He is one of the very few people in this country who have succeeded in making a living by writing for the BBC."

Indeed Durbridge continued with plays and serials for BBC radio for another thirty years, using his own name and the pseudonyms Frank Cromwell, Nicholas Vane and Lewis Middleton Harvey, but his reputation was assured when he had a brainwave that permanently defined his name. In 1938 he had the idea of creating a radio detective called Mark Conway, but soon changed his mind and hit on the dream team of novelist/detective Paul Temple and his wife Steve. This proved to be an inspired choice, as his radio serial *Send for Paul Temple* attracted over 7,000 enthusiastic listeners' letters to the BBC and led to a series that developed an impressive legion of fans in the UK and throughout Europe. In the mid-twentieth century radio detectives were extremely popular, with Paul Temple's rivals including Dick Barton (by Edward J. Mason), Philip Odell (by Lester Powell), Dr. Morelle (by Ernest Dudley), P.C. 49 (by Alan Stranks) and Ambrose West (by Philip Levene).

But Francis Durbridge turned out to be a multi-media writer. In 1952, while continuing to write for radio, he embarked on a series of BBC television serials that achieved enormous viewing figures until 1980. In fact it was his parallel television career that finally cemented his name in the history of popular culture, but he had yet another string to his bow – in 1971 in the UK, and even earlier in Germany, he turned to the theatrical stage with twist-after-twist plots in such plays *as Suddenly at Home, Murder with Love* and *House Guest*.

News of Paul Temple was broadcast from 13 November to 18 December 1939, in six twenty-five minute episodes. It was the third adventure for the Temples, with Hugh Morton as Paul and Bernadette Hodgson as Steve – the same pairing as for the first two serials the previous year, *Send for Paul Temple* and *Paul Temple and the Front Page Men*. Sir Graham Forbes of Scotland Yard was played by Lester Mudditt, who occupied this role on nineteen occasions from the initial *Send for Paul Temple* in 1938 until the final episode of *Paul Temple and the Spencer Affair* in 1958. *News of Paul Temple* clearly proved popular, and on 5 July 1944 a new production was broadcast, abridged by Durbridge to just one hour, with Richard Williams as Paul, Lucille Lisle as Steve, and Laidman Browne as Sir Graham.

The Temples acquired a huge European following, and translated radio versions of the serials were broadcast in the Netherlands from 1939, Germany from 1949, Italy from 1953 and Denmark from 1954. In the Netherlands, with Temple given a more Continental name, *News of Paul Temple* was broadcast as *Paul Vlaanderen en het Z-4 mysterie* from 14 April to 5 May 1940, translated by Willem Vogt and produced by Kommer Kleijn, with Theo Frenkel as Vlaanderen and Lily Bouwmeester as Ina. But this was Holland in wartime, and sadly Dutch listeners had to be left in suspense as only the first four episodes were broadcast. Their patience was eventually rewarded, however, because on 23 December 1946 a new 145-minute version was broadcast, translated by Willem Vogt and produced by Kommer Kleijn, with Jan van Ees as Vlaanderen and Eva Janssen as Ina.

As with its two predecessors, the radio serial *News of Paul Temple* was novelised. In May 1940 John Long published *News of Paul Temple*, written jointly by Durbridge and Charles Hatton. In Germany it has appeared as *Paul Temple und der Fall Z*, in France as *Le Tragique Rayon d'Inverdale*, in Italy as *Ritorna Paul Temple*, in the Netherlands as *Paul Vlaanderen en het Z-mysterie*, in Sweden as *Dags för Paul Temple*, and in Finland as *Mitä uutta, Paul Temple?* For lovers of UK audiobooks, it has been marketed on cassettes read by Michael Tudor Barnes (ISIS Audiobooks, 2001), on CDs read by Michael Tudor Barnes (ISIS Audiobooks, 2003) and on CDs in an abridged reading by Anthony Head (BBC Audio, 2008).

In addition the popularity of the Temples on the radio resulted in their migration to the cinema screen, with four films released between 1946 and 1952. *Paul Temple's Triumph* (Butchers/Nettlefold, 1950) was based on *News of Paul Temple*, with a screenplay by A.R. Rawlinson, produced by Ernest G. Roy and directed by Maclean Rogers. Paul and Steve were played by movie favourites John Bentley and Dinah Sheridan, and this film was marketed on DVD by Renown Pictures in 2011 and also included with the other three Temple films on the DVD set *The Paul Temple Collection Limited Edition* (Renown Pictures, 2011). It is also available as a DVD containing the English and German (dubbed) versions, *Jagd auf Z* (Pidax, 2015). The film *Paul Temple's Triumph* was released in Germany and Austria as *Jagd auf Z* and in Sweden as *Paul Temple och gäckande Z*.

So Durbridge fans will doubtless enjoy reading this script of a very early Paul Temple radio serial, maybe also ear-worming the signature tune – but make no mistake, as at the time this was a menacing extract from Rimsky-Korsakov's *Scheherazade* suite, which was used for every Temple serial until giving way in December 1947 to the more familiar *Coronation Scot* by Vivian Ellis for *Paul Temple and the Sullivan Mystery* and every serial thereafter.

Melvyn Barnes
Author of *Francis Durbridge: The Complete Guide* (Williams & Whiting 2018)

This book reproduces Francis Durbridge's original script together with the list of characters and actors of the BBC programme on the dates mentioned, but the eventual broadcast might have edited Durbridge's script in respect of scenes, dialogue and character names.

NEWS OF PAUL TEMPLE

A serial in six episodes

By FRANCIS DURBRIDGE

Broadcast on BBC Radio

November 13th – December 18th 1939

CAST:

Paul Temple	Hugh Morton
Steve, his wife	Bernadette Hodgson
Sir Graham Forbes	Lester Mudditt
An Editor	Dick Francis
Rex Bryant, a reporter	Ivan Samson
	and Maurice Denham
Dr Ludwig Steiner	Maurice Denham
	and Leo de Pokorny
Pryce	Clifford Bean
Iris Archer	Diana Morrison
Mrs Moffat	Mary O'Farrell
	and Mona Harrison
David Lindsay	Geoffrey Wincott
	and Ben Wright
Laurence van Draper	Norman Shelley
	and Bruce Winston
Major Guest	Cyril Nash
Mrs Weston	Audrey Cameron
	and Gwen Lewis
Ernie Weston	Dick Francis
Ben	Ewart Scott
Detective Inspector Fuller . . .	Alan Howland

EPISODE ONE

THE STAGE IS SET

OPEN TO: The sound of a typewriter.

EDITOR: (*Excited*) Bryant! Where the devil is Bryant?
Rex Bryant enters humming a song, at his deadpan leisure.
BRYANT: Do I hear you calling me?
EDITOR: Cut out the fooling and shut the door.
The door closes.
EDITOR: You should have been here hours ago. What the devil have you been doing?
BRYANT: I've been to the cinema. It was terrific! All about a newspaper. The editor got the scoop. The reporter got the girl. And the girl got the baby.
EDITOR: Unless you take the lead out of your pants you'll get the sack! Get down to Southampton and cover the Clipper story.
BRYANT: Come on, chief, don't make me laugh. I'm fed up with meeting film stars off planes.
EDITOR: I'm not asking you to meet film stars. Maybe you've never heard of the Golden Clipper?
BRYANT: Of course I have! New York to Southampton in sixteen hours. A nice easy flight. Where's the story in that?
EDITOR: (*Sarcastically*) I don't suppose you know by any chance who happens to be travelling on the Clipper?
BRYANT: The Quintuplets.
EDITOR: No, not the Quintuplets. Just Paul Temple. Mr and Mrs Paul Temple, to be more precise.
BRYANT: Paul Temple!!! Are you sure about that?
EDITOR: Of course I'm sure. It was in last night's Standard.
BRYANT: Well, I'm damned!

EDITOR: Do you think you could try to look a little less
            stupid by the time you arrive in Southampton?
            If you can't you'll definitely be fired. We've
            been waiting for this story to break for weeks –
            find out why Paul Temple is coming back from
            New York.

BRYANT: But everybody knows why Temple is on his
            way home.

EDITOR: Why?

BRYANT: They've been rehearsing that new play of his.
            It's due to open in a fortnight.

EDI TOR: That's old stuff! Iris Archer is taking the lead
            role, and the play is called: The Castle Lady of
            Shetland.

BRYANT: Yes. Only for some reason Iris Archer isn't
            going to be playing the part.

EDITOR: What? Why not? What's the matter with Iris
            Archer? Why isn't she playing the part?

BRYANT: I don't know. Gibson had a chat with her last
            night ... but she wouldn't say much about it.
            Just said a lot of nonsense about the part being
            unsuitable for her.

EDITOR: Well, get down to Southampton and see what
            Temple has to say about it.

BRYANT: I'd much rather go to see that new film in "The
            Empire". It's all about an editor who took the
            wrong turning.

EDITOR: (*His teeth clenched*) Are you going to
            Southampton or not ...?

BRYANT: OK, Snow White! OK! I'm going!

FADE SCENE.

4

FADE UP the sounds of a railway buffet.

STEVE: How's the circulation, Rex?

BRYANT: Not so good lately. It's the wrong time of year.

TEMPLE: It's always the wrong time of year.

BRYANT: They're sending us out after all sorts of stories that the subs slaughter down to four lines on page eight. (*To the Barman*) Another whisky, please, barman.

STEVE: What exactly are you doing down here at Southampton, Rex?

BRYANT: To be quite candid, I came down here to see your delightful husband.

TEMPLE: Things must certainly be in a bad way if I'm considered to be in the news. What's it all about?

BRYANT: Your new play for one thing. You might as well give me all the dope about it. Be a sport, Temple – a little publicity won't do the show any harm will it? Or will it?

TEMPLE: By Timothy, you boys must be hard up for news.

STEVE: Really, Rex, there's nothing to tell... If there was a story you could have it like a shot, couldn't he, darling?

TEMPLE: Like a shot! Not a word would be withheld!

BRYANT: But is Iris Archer leaving the cast, or isn't she?

TEMPLE reaches into his jacket pocket and takes out a cable.

TEMPLE: Everything I know about it you can read in this telegram. I received it shortly before we left New York.

5

BRYANT: (*Reading*) Terribly sorry unable to play Lady Seaton stop will explain later stop lots of love Iris.

TEMPLE: And a very large full stop at that.

BRYANT: But I thought you wrote the play especially for Iris Archer.

TEMPLE: Yes I did.

BRYANT: Then it strikes me as very strange –

TEMPLE: That really is all I know. Please don't ask me for anything more, Rex.

BRYANT: (*Desperate*) But look here, Temple, I have to send in some story for the paper. I can't get out of that.

STEVE: Wouldn't you be better off going and catching Sylvia Larone before she gets the train? She was on the flight as well, you know. You could ask her what she really thought of Hollywood.

BRYANT: At least tell me what your plans for the future are …

TEMPLE: We're going to Scotland for three weeks.

STEVE: You mean the South of France, dear ...

TEMPLE: (*Firmly*) To Scotland ...

STEVE: (*Equally firmly*) To the South of France ...

TEMPLE: (*Breezily*) Scotland ...

BRYANT: Ok, ok! I'll say Scotland and the South of France as far as I'm concerned. Then what?

TEMPLE: Let's see, I should have a new novel ready for Christmas. But whether ...

STEVE: We're sorry, but there's really nothing interesting to squeeze out of us, Rex. There hasn't been that! (*She snaps her fingers*). Nothing's happened at all.

BRYANT: All right, I get it. But tell me something about the trip – your personal reactions and all that sort of hot air. Did you have a good time? Who else was on board? Have a heart, you guys, I've got to turn in a couple of columns or they'll murder me.

Temple laughs.

TEMPLE: Ah! Here's Dr Steiner, he'll tell you all about the trip.... won't you, doctor?

DR LUDWIG STEINER approaches; he is an Austrian, 57 years old.

STEINER: It will be possible to get a train soon, Mr Temple?

TEMPLE: Why yes – it's due almost any minute. Then I'm afraid my wife and I shall have to leave you. We're going on by road.

STEINER: (*Sighing*) Ach, it is sad to part so soon. What a delightful journey and what interesting new impressions and experiences... What more can a man desire...? Just look at that flower in my buttonhole – the carnation is still quite fresh and bright, and to think, I bought it in New York!

BRYANT: Perhaps you wouldn't mind giving me a sort of interview, sir. Is this your first trip across the Atlantic?

TEMPLE: I should have warned you, doctor, Mr Bryant here is a representative of the London Evening Post. One of our most respected publications.

STEINER: So you are a reporter? This England becomes more like New York every day. No, young man, this was not my first trip. I have been many times before.

BRYANT: Have you any intention of visiting other European countries besides England, doctor?

STEINER: (*Quietly*) I don't know yet. That ... I will only decide later.

BRYANT: Mmmm ... I didn't quite get your name, sir?

STEINER: My name is Steiner, Dr Ludwig Steiner, Professor of Philosophy at the University of Philadelphia.

BRYANT: What's your interest in coming to Europe, doctor? Have you an interest in politics or ...?

STEINER: I am over here on holiday, my friend! Just a holiday.

FADE SCENE.

FADE IN the sound of a door opening.

PRYCE: Miss Archer is here to see you, sir.

TEMPLE: Fetch her in, please, Pryce.

A slight pause and then IRIS ARCHER enters. She is beautiful with a mysterious air about her. She acts rather sentimentally.

IRIS: Darling, how nice to see you again!

TEMPLE: Hello, Iris!

STEVE: Come in, Iris!

IRIS: Steve, my dear, you look marvellous! Doesn't she look marvellous, Paul? Now, do tell me about your trip. I'm simply dying to hear all about it. Didn't you feel scared in one of those flying machines above the water?

STEVE: A little.

IRIS: Oh, Steve, I wouldn't have lasted five minutes, I would have been absolutely petrified. The mere thought of all that water just makes me quake with fear.

TEMPLE: (*Quietly*) You look very well, Iris!

IRIS: Oh, I'm not, darling. I feel awful at times.

STEVE: Won't you take your coat off, Iris?

IRIS: No ... I won't ... I can't stay very long I'm afraid, darling ...

TEMPLE: I trust you've time for a cocktail?

IRIS: Yes. Yes, I would rather like a drink.

TEMPLE: Your favourite?

IRIS: You remember? Please, darling! Isn't he perfect, Steve? You don't know how lucky you are!

STEVE laughs.

TEMPLE starts to pour drinks.

IRIS: Paul, did you get my telegram?

TEMPLE: Yes. I got it just before we left New York. It was handed to me just as we were getting on the plane.

IRIS: Were you ... were you ... surprised?

TEMPLE: Actually, yes ... (*A short pause*) Iris, are you serious about this?

IRIS: (*Grimly*) I don't think I've ever been quite so serious in my life before.

STEVE: (*Confused*) But why? What's the matter? Has Seaman been nasty about something?

IRIS: No, no, it's not that. Oh no, he's a great director.

TEMPLE: Here we are, Iris. Here's your drink.

IRIS: Thank you, darling.

TEMPLE: Steve.

STEVE: Thank you.

They all drink.

TEMPLE: Is it money? Is that the problem? I thought we'd offered you a splendid contract. After all, we gave way to you over that film business.

IRIS: (*Without conviction*) I'm sorry, Paul, but I've been badly miscast.

9

TEMPLE: (*Surprised; laughing*) Come off it, Iris, that's ridiculous! You said yourself that the role fitted you like a glove.

IRIS: (*Quietly*) That ... that was six weeks ago, when I said that.

STEVE: Aren't you feeling very well, Iris?

IRIS: Well ... honestly ... not terribly, darling

TEMPLE: What are you going to do instead? Make a film?

IRIS: No. I'm – well, I'm going to the South of France for a month or two. Then when I come back ... then ... I might go back to work. I don't know – yet.

TEMPLE: Are you going alone?

IRIS: Yes ... Quite alone ...

STEVE: Where abouts on the Riviera are you going to stay? Paul and I are thinking about ...

IRIS: Oh, a small village, near St Maxim ... it's very quiet. Hardly anyone knows about it.

TEMPLE: Well, I'm very sorry about all this.

IRIS: You're very sweet about it.

TEMPLE: I suppose there isn't a chance that you might still change your mind, Iris? As far as the play is concerned, I mean.

IRIS: No ... no ... I'm afraid there isn't, darling.

TEMPLE: Iris, do you mind if I tell you something quite frankly?

IRIS: Oh not at all, Paul. No, of course not. Provided of course you don't ... get too candid ...

STEVE laughs.

TEMPLE: Six months ago, you wrote me a letter about the play. You said you found it well written, very amusing and that the role of Lady Seaton was quite the best part offered you for many years.

10

IRIS:	Oh yes, I did. I remember the letter perfectly. And I meant it, Paul. Every word of it. Really, I was quite sincere.
TEMPLE:	Yes. Yes, I know you were. I'm convinced of that.
IRIS:	What do you mean?
TEMPLE:	Iris, why are you leaving the cast? It's not because you don't like the play any longer. I know you well enough to realise you wouldn't change your mind. It's not because the part doesn't suit you. You've got another and more important reason, haven't you?
IRIS:	Yes, but ... but ... it's really no use, asking me what that reason is, because I can't tell you.
TEMPLE:	How about if we postponed the performance of the play for a few months? Would that suit you?
IRIS:	You mean, would I still want to play Lady Seaton if you held the role for me until .... well, let's say just before Christmas ?
TEMPLE:	Yes, that's what I mean.
IRIS:	But Paul, you can't make a decision like that – not by yourself!
TEMPLE:	You haven't answered my question.
IRIS:	Oh, I would love to do it, Paul, to be able to play the part. It's a lovely play and a wonderful role for me, but –
TEMPLE:	But what, Iris? .... There's always a but!
IRIS:	But I must be free between now and the tenth of November.
TEMPLE:	All right, then that's settled. I'll write to Seaman tonight.

IRIS: (*Pleased*) Paul, you are a downright darling!
             The very idea of having to relinquish the role of
             Lady Seaton nearly broke my heart.
STEVE: (*Laughing*) Go ahead and kiss him, Iris.
IRIS: You don't know what a weight you've taken
             off my mind, Paul. Now I really must fly!
STEVE: When are you leaving?
IRIS: On Saturday.
TEMPLE: And can I write to Seaman then, and tell him
             that you will be back in town before the end of
             November?
IRIS: Not a day later than the seventeenth of
             November, darling! I promise.
TEMPLE: Good. Now take care of yourself, Iris. I don't
             want to hear of any accidents happening to my
             leading lady.
IRIS: (*Cheerfully*) I will. I promise!
The door opens. PRYCE enters.
PRYCE: Sir Graham Forbes is here to see you, sir.
TEMPLE: (*Surprised*) Sir Graham Forbes?
PRYCE: Yes, sir.
STEVE: (*Startled*) Paul!
TEMPLE: (*Laughing*) It's all right, darling. It's nothing.
             Absolutely nothing for you to get excited
             about.
IRIS: Sir Graham Forbes ... doesn't he have
             something to do with Scotland Yard or
             something?
TEMPLE: (*Amused*) He's Scotland Yard itself! Pryce, will
             you please take Miss Archer to her car?
PRYCE: Yes, sir
TEMPLE: Then you can show Sir Graham in.
PRYCE: Very good, sir. (*To IRIS*) This door, miss, if
             you please.

IRIS:	Well, bye Paul, and thank you again for being so understanding. You are a darling! You really are! Bye, Steve, goodbye!
STEVE:	Bye, Iris, take care!
TEMPLE:	Bye, Iris, have a good trip! I'll write to Seaman tonight.
IRIS:	Do! Bye!

The door closes after IRIS and PRYCE go out.

| STEVE: | (*Annoyed*) Paul, if Sir Graham is here because .... because he needs your help, then please – |

The door opens suddenly and SIR GRAHAM FORBES enters.

FORBES:	(*Entering, quietly*) Sir Graham is here because he needs a cocktail. A very strong cocktail. And nothing else, Mrs Temple!
STEVE:	(*Surprised*) Why, Sir Graham!
TEMPLE:	(*Laughing*) Come along in, Sir Graham. It's good to see you again.
STEVE:	Didn't Pryce ...
FORBES:	Yes, Pryce wanted to announce me all right. But he seemed to have his hands more than full with that blonde female.
TEMPLE:	That was Iris Archer ... You've probably heard of her.
FORBES:	Iris Archer! She is extraordinarily good looking, isn't she?
TEMPLE:	Yes, she is! What would you like to drink, Sir Graham? Sherry, Bronx, Sidecar?
FORBEs:	I'd rather like a Bronx, if you don't mind, Temple.
TEMPLE:	A Bronx, excellent.

TEMPLE starts to pour more drinks.

13

FORBES: What was the trip like, Temple? Got a bit of a shock when I heard you were coming over on the Clipper.

STEVE: Oh, it was wonderful, Sir Graham! We enjoyed every minute of it, didn't we, darling?

PAUL: Every minute! Here's your cocktail, Sir Graham.

FORBES: Thank you

STEVE: I'll have a sherry, dear.

PAUL: Sherry, coming right up.

FORBES: Is that Iris ... what's her name again ...

PAUL: You mean Iris Archer?

FORBES: Yes, that's right. Isn't she going into a play of yours? I seem to remember reading something about it.

PAUL: Well, she was going into a play of mine. Now things seem a little uncertain.

FORBES: Oh, that's a shame.

PAUL: Here's your sherry, darling.

STEVE: Thank you, Paul.

TEMPLE: And what is Scotland Yard doing at the moment, Sir Graham?

FORBES: Well, just at the moment we are up against one of the greatest criminal organisations –

STEVE: (*Annoyed*) What?!!

FORBES: (*Amused*) Oh dear, what have I said – the look on your face, Steve!

TEMPLE: Sir Graham's only pulling your leg, darling. Don't worry.

STEVE: You're a very wicked man, Sir Graham!

FORBES: (*Laughs at his successful joke*) As a matter of fact, Temple, things are pretty dead. They have been for months. One or two isolated murders, but nothing really big since The Front Page

14

Men, and I can't honestly say I'm sorry. (*He finishes his drink*) I must be on my way – I only dropped in to welcome the wanderers home again.

TEMPLE: We're going away again in a day or two, but when we get back you must come to dinner and –

FORBES: I shall be out of town myself for about a month. First holiday I've taken for nearly six years.

TEMPLE: Really? Where are you going?

FORBES: Carol's taken a villa just outside Nice.

STEVE: Nice?

FORBES: Yes. I say, you two don't happen to be going to the South of France, by any chance?

TEMPLE: (*Amused*) Oddly enough, Sir Graham –

STEVE: We're going to Scotland.

TEMPLE: Scotland!

STEVE: (*Sweetly*) You did want to go to Scotland, didn't you, darling?

TEMPLE: Why – er – yes. Yes, of course.

STEVE: Then that's fine.

TEMPLE: (*Surprised*) But I …

FORBES: (*Laughing*) To Scotland or the South of France, it doesn't matter, Temple, where you go. As long as you're careful not to get caught up in some shady business that needs unravelling.

STEVE: He won't get a chance to do that. That is precisely the reason why we are going to Scotland. Nothing criminal ever happens there.

They all laugh.
FADE SCENE.

FADE UP the sound of a car travelling at a moderate speed. The weather is very bad, we hear the sound of thunder and driving rain followed by a fierce clap of thunder.

STEVE: (*Startled*) Paul!

TEMPLE: Don't worry, darling. It was just a clap of thunder.

STEVE: The rain seems to be getting worse.

TEMPLE: The sky's certainly still pretty dark overhead.

There is another thunderclap.

STEVE: It's not so dark in that direction. And I don't believe the lightning is quite so bad now.

TEMPLE: Perhaps not. (*Pause*) I say, this road is terrible. It's full of potholes! All we need now is to get a puncture and everything in the garden will be lovely!

STEVE: How far are we from Inverdale now?

TEMPLE: I'm beginning to seriously doubt that such a place still exists in Scotland.

STEVE: There must be, darling. It's on the map.

TEMPLE: But it's a very old map, Steve. (*He laughs*) Hello, what's this?

STEVE: It looks like some village or other.

TEMPLE: I hope this isn't Inverdale.

STEVE: It can't be, darling. There's nothing except cottages.

The car slows down.

TEMPLE: At least the storm seems to have passed over now.

STEVE: Thank goodness for that. Still, I would like to know where we actually are.

TEMPLE: Yes. We need to know that first, because there's no point in going on if we're on the wrong road.

STEVE: Let me look at the map again.

The car stops.

16

STEVE:	What time is it, darling?
TEMPLE:	It's just half past six. The time we've been going I thought it was much later.
STEVE:	Look, Paul, this is the road we took from Edinburgh. We must have done two hundred miles by now.
TEMPLE:	Just a minute, Steve, that second house looks like a shop by the looks of things. Hopefully they can put us on the right track.
STEVE:	Yes, it might be quicker to ask.
TEMPLE:	OK. I won't be a minute. You stay in the car.
STEVE:	All right. Get some chocolate, darling – fruit and nut for me.
TEMPLE:	Wouldn't you also like a tender steak with some sauté potatoes?

TEMPLE starts to get out of the car.

| STEVE: | What? And no onions? |

They both laugh at the idea.
The car door closes.
PAUL TEMPLE walks towards the shop.
He opens the door and a shop bell rings as he does so.
The door closes.
Mrs Moffat appears. She is a middle-aged woman with a monotone voice.

MRS MOFFAT:	Good evening.
TEMPLE:	Oh, good evening.
MRS MOFFAT:	What can I get ye?
TEMPLE:	I should like some chocolates please.
MRS MOFFAT:	We don't keep chocolates.
TEMPLE:	Oh, I see. Very well, I'll have some postcards then.
MRS MOFFAT:	Single ones or a packet?

TEMPLE: Yes, just give me that packet.

MRS MOFFAT: Six beautiful photographs of Inverdale. Two were taken by moonlight. That will be sixpence.

TEMPLE produces a coin.

TEMPLE: Thank you.

MRS MOFFAT: I'll just put them in an envelope for you.

TEMPLE: Er – yes, thank you.

A short pause.

TEMPLE: How far is Inverdale from here?

MRS MOFFAT: Just about two miles.

TEMPLE: (*Pleased*) Oh good. I thought it was further than that.

MRS MOFFAT: No, no more than two miles (*She accepts the money*) Thank you.

MRS MOFFAT opens a drawer and puts the money in it. She closes the drawer sharply.

TEMPLE: I don't suppose you know a decent hotel in Inverdale, by any chance?

MRS MOFFAT: (*After a moment's thought*) Well, there is an inn.

TEMPLE: (*Doing his best to be as friendly as possible*) I hope it's a good one.

MRS MOFFAT: (*Taking Paul's best interest*) Not bad – it's not at all bad.

TEMPLE: Should I just keep going straight on from here, or is there another way, which I should.... (*He hesitates, being surprised by MRS MOFFAT's attitude*)

MRS MOFFAT: (*Pretending not to have heard anything*) Ye're a stranger round these parts?

TEMPLE: Yes, very much so, I'm afraid.

MRS MOFFAT: Have ye come far?

TEMPLE: London.

MRS MOFFAT:	London? That's a long way.
TEMPLE:	Yes.
MRS MOFFAT:	I've a married sister in London. In Peckham, I believe. Would there be a place called Peckham?
TEMPLE:	Yes, there's a place called Peckham.
MRS MOFFAT:	(*Sighing*) Huh, it must be a wonderful thing to travel! Very often I've wished I had the time, an' the money o' course! What was it Shakespeare said about travellers?
TEMPLE:	As far as I can gather, he said quite a number of things.
MRS MOFFAT:	(*Coolly, as if they hadn't been talking together*) Here's your change.
TEMPLE:	Thank you.
MRS MOFFAT:	H'm – will ye be wanting anything else now?

The shop door opens and the bell rings.

DAVID LINDSAY enters. He is a lively young man of about twenty-eight. He's out of breath.

MRS MOFFAT:	Why, Mr Lindsay!
LINDSAY:	Hello, Mrs Moffat.
MRS MOFFAT:	Gracious me, ye've certainly been running!
LINDSAY:	I'm sorry for bursting in here like this. (*To TEMPLE*) No, please don't go, sir. (*He continues gasping for breath*)
TEMPLE:	Apart from being out of breath, you seem to be rather excited about something. Is something wrong? Has something happened?
LINDSAY:	I saw your car go by about a quarter of a mile back. Then I saw you stop at Mrs

	Moffat's shop, so I raced along after you. I was afraid you might get started again before ... before I could get here and have a word with you.
TEMPLE:	With me? Can I help you at all?
LINDSAY:	I was wondering if you happened to be going to Inverdale.
TEMPLE:	Yes, as a matter of fact I am on my way to Inverdale.
LINDSAY:	Ah ... Then would you be good enough to do me a favour?
TEMPLE:	Well, I might. It all depends on what it is. What is it exactly?
LINDSAY:	Well, there's an inn in Inverdale called The Royal Gate. I don't know if you know it or not?
TEMPLE:	As a matter of fact my wife and I intend spending the night at Inverdale, so –
LINDSAY:	Oh, but that's splendid! Well, look here, you can do me a great favour. When you get to The Royal Gate would you be so kind as to ask there for a certain Mr John Richmond, and then ... (*His voice becomes tense*) And then, will you please give him (*His voice changes to a whisper*) this letter?
TEMPLE:	Mr John Richmond? (*Suddenly*) But of course, with the greatest pleasure. Just give me the letter.

LINDSAY hands TEMPLE the letter who studies it thoughtfully.

| LINDSAY: | (*Seriously*) Please realise that this is most important. Under no circumstances must |

	you give the letter to anyone else. Do you understand, under no circumstances!
TEMPLE:	But suppose this Mr Richmond doesn't happen to be staying at the inn?
LINDSAY:	He'll be there all right.
TEMPLE:	(*After a short pause*) A moment ago, you said that you saw my car pass a quarter of a mile back. Why didn't you stop me then?
LINDSAY:	I only saw your headlights, and I was afraid you might be ... someone else...
TEMPLE:	Someone else? (*Suddenly*) Well, don't worry about the letter. I'll see that friend of yours gets it all right. It's a straight road into the village, I gather?
LINDSAY:	Perfectly. You can't possibly go wrong. The Royal Gate is on the left hand side, about halfway down the main street.
TEMPLE:	Thanks. Good evening to you both!

TEMPLE opens the shop door and the bell rings.

MRS MOFFAT:	(*Quietly*) Ye're forgetting your postcards.
TEMPLE:	Oh yes, silly me. Thank you. Good evening!

TEMPLE leaves and the door closes.

LINDSAY:	(*Still excited*) Mrs Moffat, if it's not too much to ask, could I use your phone for a moment? I just need to...
MRS MOFFAT:	I'm very sorry, Mr Lindsay, but the telephone's out of order. It has been ever since yon storm started.
LINDSAY:	Oh ... (*A short pause*) I see. It's out of order ...

MRS MOFFAT: Ye can try if ye like, of course, but I don't think ye'll succeed. The wires must have broken somewhere.

LINDSAY: (*Thinking of something else*) Oh ... yes ... of course ... yes... yes... thank you...

MRS MOFFAT: Is there anything else I can do for you, Mr Lindsay? Otherwise, I'll just go into the back by the fire.

LINDSAY: No ... no, I'm afraid you can't do anything. Thanks all the same. Good evening, Mrs Moffat!

MRS MOFFAT: Good evening, Mr Lindsay!

Door opens and closes as LINDSAY leaves, shop bell rings. There is a brief pause.

A telephone is taken off the hook.

MRS MOFFAT: Hello, I want Inverdale 74 ...Hello, hello, is it you? ... (*Suddenly*) Yes... Yes – he's been here. Just left ... No. No, I couldn't ... Wait a minute, for God's sake listen to me, he gave a letter to a man who happened to be here ... (*Impatiently*) Well alrighty, now listen to what I'm saying for a moment! (*Quietly*) It was addressed to a Mr John Richmond at The Royal Gate.

MRS MOFFAT replaces the telephone receiver.

FADE SCENE.

FADE IN dramatic incidental music.

FADE music.

FADE IN the sound of a car travelling at a moderate speed.

STEVE: I don't know about you, darling, but the two miles to Inverdale seem like awfully long miles!

22

TEMPLE: I was just thinking the same thing, Steve.

A pause.

STEVE: That young man seemed to be in rather a hurry, don't you think?

TEMPLE: (*Quietly*) You mean the young man who gave me the letter?

STEVE: Yes. He came running down the road as if his life depended on it. At first I thought there had been an accident!

TEMPLE: It's rather off ... He said he saw the car a quarter of a mile back before we stopped at the shop.

STEVE: Then why didn't he stop us?

TEMPLE: Yes, that's exactly what I wanted to know from him too. (*Pause*) Apparently he was afraid we were someone else. After all, he couldn't see anything but our headlights.

With thunderous speed, a second car approaches.

TEMPLE: By Timothy, this fellow's in a hurry. Bloody hell! Is that guy all...

STEVE: (*Excitedly*) He wants to get in front of you, Paul!

TEMPLE: Get in front of me? What the blazes does he think he's doing, damn fool!

STEVE: He wants you to stop, darling.

TEMPLE: Stop?

STEVE: Yes, he's making signs.

There is an awful squeal of brakes. Both cars come to a standstill.

TEMPLE: Those men must have lost their way.

STEVE: I think there are two of them.

TEMPLE: Fancy them pulling in front of me like that. There's no way I can pass them.

We hear footsteps. Two men appear.

23

VAN DRAPER:	(*Rather too extravagantly*) Really, sir, I must apologise for stopping you like this.
STEVE:	(*Pleasantly*) If you want the road to Inverdale –
VAN DRAPER:	Unfortunately, madam, we are not interested in the road to Inverdale.
GUEST:	(*Quietly*) I think perhaps we had better introduce ourselves, Laurence.
VAN DRAPER:	Why, yes, of course! I had overlooked that! My name is van Draper, Dr Laurence van Draper. This gentleman is Major Lindsay, a very close friend of mine. In fact, he is the father of that excitable young man you met in the village – about ten minutes ago.
TEMPLE:	I see.
GUEST:	I believe I am correct in saying my son gave you a letter.
TEMPLE:	Yes, that's quite true.
GUEST:	The letter was addressed to a certain Mr John Richmond.
TEMPLE:	Well?
GUEST:	I would esteem it a favour if you would be so kind as to give the letter to Dr van Draper.

A pause.

TEMPLE:	I'm really sorry, Major, but your son gave me explicit instructions that the letter was to be delivered to no one except Mr Richmond.
GUEST:	I'm afraid your task will be very difficult, sir. You see, there is no such person as Mr John Richmond.
TEMPLE:	No such person?

VAN DRAPER: Perhaps you'd better let me explain, Major. Look here, sir, David Lindsay, the young man who gave you that letter, is unfortunately the victim of a rather unusual ... yes ... how shall I call it ... mental condition.

STEVE: You mean he is not right in the head?

VAN DRAPER: That is to say, ma'am, he cannot be held entirely responsible for some of his actions. Oh, fundamentally there is no real harm in the boy and we know he is progressing nicely at the moment, compared to before, but at times, and tonight was one of them I'm afraid - he had such a fit again – when he's a little – er – unbalanced.

TEMPLE: I understand perfectly.

VAN DRAPER: My treatment of this case is of a purely psychological nature and for that reason alone I would appreciate receiving that letter back. But if you feel even the slightest doubt about whether you can hand it over ...

TEMPLE: Oh, no, of course not, doctor. There is no question of doubting your word. But ... tell me, how do you actually know about the letter?

A pause.

GUEST: Mrs Moffat rang us up. She knows all about David's little weaknesses and she understands ...

TEMPLE: Oh, yes – of course. Sure ... Right, right ... Of course ... Mrs Moffat ... Here's the letter!

25

GUEST:	Thank you. And now I'll move my car out of the way so you can get by. I seem to have taken up all the road.
TEMPLE:	(*Amused*) Yes, you have rather, haven't you?
VAN DRAPER:	Good evening. Thank you very much! Goodbye, madam.
STEVE:	Goodbye!

The car drives away.

General evening sounds are heard.

The car drives faster.

There is a long pause, during which nothing is said.

Then Paul starts laughing to himself.

STEVE:	Paul, what's the matter? What are you laughing at?
TEMPLE:	Have you ever in your life heard such a ridiculous story?
STEVE:	What the doctor said you mean?
PAUL:	The doctor? He's no more a doctor than I am. The fellow didn't look like a doctor at all and, by Timothy, he certainly didn't talk like one!
STEVE:	But if you didn't believe his story, why did you give him the letter?
TEMPLE:	I didn't give him the letter, darling! I gave him the postcards. Six beautiful pictures of Inverdale. Two taken by moonlight!

TEMPLE continues to laugh.

FADE SCENE.

FADE IN incidental music.

FADE music.

FADE IN a door opening.

ERNIE and Mrs WESTON enter; he speaks a dialect.

MRS WESTON: I think you'll be very comfortable 'ere. It may not be as palatial as some of these railway hotels, but the view's a champion anyway.

STEVE: Oh, thank you! We'll be fine with this. This room will do very nicely, thanks.

ERNIE: (*Rather out of breath*) Where should I put these, madam? I'll bring the other suitcases later.

TEMPLE: That's all right, leave it to me. I'll take care of that.

ERNIE: Thank you, sir.

STEVE: You seem to be rather busy here. Is it always like this?

ERNIE: Goodness gracious no. This place was a proper white elephant up till a couple o' months ago. Ain't that right, mother?

MRS WESTON: Well, things 'ave bucked up, there's no doubt about that.

ERNIE: Listen to her! Bucked up! Blimey, I should think they 'ave. I've been run off me feet for weeks from early morning till last thing at night. 'Ave you come far, sir?

TEMPLE: We left Edinburgh at about ten o'clock this morning.

ERNIE: Well, that's a long way! You made pretty good goin'. I expect you're feelin' a bit peckish?

STEVE: Yes, we are rather.

ERNIE: Well then, madam and sir, we eat at half past seven. Don't worry about it. You just listen for the gong. Yes, sir, we are proud of that gong, just like a real hotel! That's mother's idea.

MRS WESTON:	Yes, lately we have had so many fine ladies and gentlemen here that I thought we should make sure they had it here as they were used to at home. Shall I get you water and a clean towel, madam, so you can freshen up a bit?
STEVE:	That would be lovely! Thank you.
MRS WESTON:	Then perhaps I can take you along to the bathroom?
STEVE:	Thank you. I won't be long, Paul!
TEMPLE:	O.K.!

The door is closed.

ERNIE:	Well, then, I'll just go down, sir, to get the rest of the luggage. When I've done that then ...
TEMPLE:	No, wait a minute. This inn here, is it run by you and your wife?
ERNIE:	So it is, sir. Weston is my name. Ernie, that's me and Molly Weston, that's my wife. We've been here two years now. Two tough years, sir, I can tell you.
TEMPLE:	You don't seem to like it very much.
ERNIE:	Oh well, these days it's all right. Business is a tad better. But boy, it's a struggle to keep going!
TEMPLE:	The hotel seems pretty full at the moment.
ERNIE:	Not 'arf. Everybody seems to 'ave made their minds up to go on 'oliday just now. Between you and me, sir, you wouldn't be 'aving this room if me and the missus weren't pally.
TEMPLE:	Have you anyone staying here named Richmond – John Richmond?

ERNIE: (*Surprised*) Why, yes, sir! Is 'e a pal o' yours?

TEMPLE: No, but I'd like a word with him.

ERNIE: Well, I think 'e's out, sir. But 'e'll soon be back for dinner.

TEMPLE: Good. I'll see him then. Here, that's for you.

TEMPLE gives ERNIE a tip.

ERNIE: Thank you very much, sir. If you need anything else just ask me, ok? And if you fancy anythin' tasty-like for dinner, just tell the missis.

TEMPLE: (*Chuckling*) Thank you. I will.

ERNIE goes and the door closes.

TEMPLE opens his suitcase and whistles a tune to himself as he starts to unpack.

There is a knock on the door.

TEMPLE: Come in!

The door opens and DR STEINER enters.

STEINER: I trust I do not intrude, Mr Temple?

TEMPLE: (*Surprised*) Why, Dr Steiner! Come in, doctor, come in!!!

STEINER: I saw your name in the register and I couldn't resist the opportunity of renewing our... our... transatlantic friendship! (*He laughs*)

TEMPLE: It's delightful to see you again. But I am surprised. What are you doing in Scotland?

STEINER: I am on holiday and I'm trying as hard as I can to forget that I'm a professor of philosophy at Philadelphia University. But it's not easy, I'm afraid. These Scottish people are very interesting to a philosopher. They are in many ways highly religious and, shall we say, narrow-minded. And yet they worship their national poet, Robert Burns. You have, no doubt, heard of Burns?

TEMPLE: (*Chuckling*) Yes, I've heard of Rabbie Burns.

STEINER: And yet again the Scottish race frown upon divorce. They look upon marriage as sacred, binding and eternal. Yet it is easier to divorce in Scotland than anywhere else in the British Isles. Perhaps, you can explain these inconsistencies, Mr Temple. I should be most happy to listen and to take notes.

The door is opened.

STEVE enters; she is excited.

STEVE: Paul, the most amazing thing –

STEVE stops speaking as soon as she sees STEINER is in the room.

STEVE: Oh, good heavens, Dr Steiner! What are you doing here?

TEMPLE: (*Laughing*) You are as surprised as I was, Steve, and no wonder! Who was expecting Dr Steiner to be here? Dr Steiner has just arrived, dear. He saw our name in the register.

STEINER: Quite possibly I am wasting my talents on philosophy. I could much better have become a detective! But then I was still misled, because surely you told me on the plane that you shortly leave for the South of France...

STEVE: Paul suddenly changed his mind. He thought it would be too hot there.

TEMPLE: I like that, I must say!

STEINER: (*Laughs*) I am glad to see a man change his mind. Well, one thing is certain, in Scotland, you won't find it too hot. B-r-r! Nowhere have I felt as cold as here, not even in Philadelphia!

STEVE laughs.

TEMPLE: How long are you staying here, doctor?

STEINER: I don't actually know ... It depends, you see... Depends a lot on the weather ... But come, I must go and unpack my bags now. We shall meet later, I hope – at dinner?

TEMPLE: Why, yes, of course. You must sit at our table. I'll arrange it.

STEINER: I shall be honoured. Then for the time being … auf wiedersehen!

STEINER leaves and the door is closed.

STEVE: Oh now, Paul, I have something to tell you that will amaze you. I don't know how I managed to keep it to myself whilst Dr Steiner was here!

TEMPLE: Calm down, Steve, calm down! What on earth is this all about? You came dashing in here as if all the Campbells and McLeods were after you.

STEVE: Paul, you'll never guess who I just saw here in the hotel.

TEMPLE: I haven't the vaguest idea.

STEVE: Iris!

TEMPLE: (*Amazed*) Iris? Here in the hotel?

STEVE: Yes, dear.

TEMPLE: Now don't be silly, Steve, you can't! She's in the South of France!

STEVE: (*Seriously*) Really, Paul, I'm not joking. I really have seen Iris. I just stepped out of the bathroom and at the other end of the corridor a door opened and … who do you think came out? None other than Iris! Can you imagine how surprised I was?

TEMPLE: Did she see you?

STEVE: (*Pondering*) I don't actually know ... But I have a feeling that she did.

TEMPLE: But – but what happened? Where did she go?

STEVE: Well, there's a staircase at the end of the corridor, near her room. Before I could say

	anything she had turned her back to me and disappeared.
TEMPLE:	Why didn't you call to her?
STEVE:	I was so startled – it was like one of those dreams when you feel quite helpless.
TEMPLE:	It's certainly very peculiar. What the devil would Iris be doing here?

The gong for dinner is heard in the background.

STEVE:	Oh dear, there's the gong already and we haven't even started unpacking our suitcases!
TEMPLE:	That's darned odd about Iris! I wonder if...
STEVE:	(*Quickly*) Paul!
TEMPLE:	Yes, Steve?
STEVE:	Paul, I've just remembered about that letter. Hadn't you better inquire –?
TEMPLE:	I already have.
STEVE:	Then there is a John Richmond?
TEMPLE:	There certainly is. And he's staying here at this very hotel.

A short pause.

STEVE:	(*Rather confused*) Paul, you don't think...
TEMPLE:	Think what, dear?
STEVE:	Oh nothing...
TEMPLE:	Go on, Steve, what were you about to say?
STEVE:	I was about to say: surely you don't think that there is any connection between those two men who stopped our car ... that young man who gave you the letter ... and Iris? And yes, come to think of it, and actually also with Dr Steiner?
TEMPLE:	(*In thought*) I don't know ...

There is a knock on the door.

TEMPLE:	Come in.

The door opens and ERNIE WESTON enters.

ERNIE: Excuse me, sir, but you wanted me to let you know when Mr Richmond returned. I've brought him upstairs to see you.

TEMPLE: Oh, right ... Of course ...! Thank you. Ask Mr Richmond to come in immediately.

ERNIE: Very good, sir. (*In the corridor*) This way, sir!

A short pause.

TEMPLE: Why, Mr ...

STEVE: (*Astonished*) Sir Graham! What are you doing here?

TEMPLE: (*Surprised*) Sir Graham! By Timothy, Sir Graham, what on earth are you doing here?

FORBES: (*Quietly*) There seems to be some mistake ... My name is Richmond. John Richmond ...

FADE UP closing music.

END OF EPISODE ONE

EPISODE TWO

CONCERNING Z.4

OPEN TO:

STEVE: (*Rather confused*) Paul, you don't think...
TEMPLE: Think what, dear?
STEVE: Oh nothing...
TEMPLE: Go on, Steve, what were you about to say?
STEVE: I was about to say: surely you don't think that there is any connection between those two men who stopped our car ... that young man who gave you the letter ... and Iris? And yes, come to think of it, and actually also with Dr Steiner?
TEMPLE: (*In thought*) I don't know ...

There is a knock on the door.

TEMPLE: Come in.

The door opens and ERNIE WESTON enters.

ERNIE: Excuse me, sir, but you wanted me to let you know when Mr Richmond returned. I've brought him upstairs to see you.
TEMPLE: Oh, right ... Of course ...! Thank you. Ask Mr Richmond to come in immediately.
ERNIE: Very good, sir. (*In the corridor*) This way, sir!

A short pause.

TEMPLE: Why, Mr ...
STEVE: (*Astonished*) Sir Graham! What are you doing here?
TEMPLE: (*Surprised*) Sir Graham! By Timothy, Sir Graham, what on earth are you doing here?
FORBES: (*Quietly*) There seems to be some mistake ... My name is Richmond. John Richmond ...
TEMPLE: Really, sir, we must beg your forgiveness. By Timothy, I've never seen anything like it ... The same chin, the same nose ... Why, he's just like old Forbes, isn't he, Steve? The

37

	absolute spit of old Forbes – just look at his hair … well, I'm damned!
FORBES:	What the devil is this all about? Who are this lady and gentleman?
ERNIE:	A Mr and Mrs Temple, sir. Arrived about half an hour ago. (*An awkward pause*) There seems to have been some sort of mistake, doesn't there?
FORBES:	I thought you said they wanted to see me.
ERNIE:	Well, 'e said 'e did want to see you. I say, what's the game? You said I was to give a message to …
TEMPLE:	(*Laughing*) It's all right, Mr Weston. There's nothing to get excited about. This gentleman reminded us of someone else, that's all.
ERNIE:	(*A little shaken up*) But this is the gent you wanted to see – Mr Richmond –
TEMPLE:	It's all perfectly clear, Mr Weston, don't worry. The thing is, we've never met Mr Richmond before and now it turns out that he is so terribly similar to a close acquaintance of ours. It's really quite amazing the similarity.
FORBES:	This is all very well, but I'm afraid I haven't got time for all this, so if you would be so kind …
TEMPLE:	Oh, please excuse me. Allow me to introduce myself. My name is … (*Suddenly*) It's all right, Weston, thank you, there's no need for you to stay any longer.
ERNIE:	Well, don't forget, we don't serve dinner after a quarter to.
TEMPLE:	Don't worry. We won't forget.
ERNIE:	I'll be going then.
TEMPLE:	Thank you again.

ERNIE leaves and the door closes.

There is a short pause whilst they wait to make sure ERNIE is out of the way.

TEMPLE: Sir Graham, I'm most terribly sorry. It was extremely stupid of us both to blurt out your name like that.

FORBES: That's all right. You covered it up well enough. But what the devil are you two doing here?

TEMPLE: Well, if it comes to that –

FORBES: I know! I know! Don't ask me, Temple. Don't ask me! But seriously, what made you two visit Inverdale? You couldn't have had an inkling … it isn't possible …

STEVE: But we did tell you we were coming to Scotland.

FORBES: So you did. Yes, I'd forgotten about that.

TEMPLE: Sir Graham, don't you think you might tell us why you are staying here under the name of Richmond?

FORBES: Yes, that's another thing, Temple. You asked to see Mr John Richmond. I am John Richmond, though how the devil –

STEVE: Paul, give him the letter. Then we can go down to dinner.

FORBES: What letter?

TEMPLE: A letter from a young man named Lindsay – David Lindsay.

FORBES: (*Surprised*) For me?

TEMPLE: Yes.

FORBES: I don't know anyone named Lindsay, David Lindsay. There must be some mistake.

STEVE: (*Amazed*) You don't know anyone called Lindsay?

FORBES: No

39

STEVE: Is there another John Richmond staying here?

FORBES: Not that I know of.

STEVE: Then this letter must be for you.

TEMPLE: This gets brighter and brighter! First of all I meet the delightful Mrs Moffat, then the excitable Mr Lindsay, and later –

FORBES: (*Surprised*) Mrs Moffat? You mean the woman in the village shop?

TEMPLE: That's right. The dark-eyed beauty with a sister in Peckham.

FORBES: How did you meet Mrs Moffat?

STEVE: On our way here, Sir Graham, we got lost. We stopped in the village, and to make absolutely certain of getting on the right road for Inverdale Paul went into the shop to check.

TEMPLE: I popped into Mrs Moffat's. Just as I was on the verge of leaving, in barged the young fellow I was telling you about – David Lindsay. He was obviously excited and rather worried about something. To cut a long story short, he asked me if I was coming into Inverdale, and whether I'd deliver a letter for him to a Mr John Richmond, who happened to be staying at The Royal Gate. Naturally, I agreed to do so. On the way here, however, two men stopped us –

FORBES: Can you describe them?

TEMPLE: There was a man who called himself Doctor Laurence van Draper, and another, rather military-looking chap, who said that he was Major Lindsay, father of the young man who gave me the letter. They told us a rather one-sided story about the young fellow being a bit mental, and more or less demanded the letter.

They were quite nice about it, but obviously meant business.

FORBES: (*Hugely interested*) What happened?

STEVE: Well, Paul happened to buy a packet of post cards, which Mrs Moffat fortunately popped into an envelope.

FORBES: You don't mean to say you gave them the postcards?

TEMPLE: Yes I'm afraid so.

FORBES: Well, I'm damned! Now listen, Temple, this is most important. I want you to describe that young man as closely as possible.

TEMPLE: Lindsay, you mean? Oh, he was about five feet ten – dark – good-looking –

STEVE: Rather like Frank Lawton, the film actor.

FORBES: (*Excited*) My God, it's Hammond all right! Noel Hammond. Now, of course, I understand.

STEVE: Darling, what is it?

TEMPLE: (*Baffled*) The letter … Something has happened to the letter.

STEVE: The letter!

FORBES: (*Dreading the worst*) Temple, you don't mean to say –

TEMPLE: It's gone.

STEVE: Gone! But, Paul, it couldn't possibly –

FORBES: You didn't make a mistake about those postcards, Temple?

TEMPLE: No. I had the letter when I arrived here. I'm absolutely certain of that. When I was unpacking, I changed into this old sports coat and left the other on the chair.

FORBES: That letter's important, Temple. It's desperately important, and we've got to get it back.

41

TEMPLE: Those men – van Draper and the fellow who called himself Major Lindsay – they must have contacted someone here at The Royal Gate.

FORBES: Yes, I agree.

STEVE: But even so, I don't see how that letter could have been taken from in here.

FORBES: Who did you see when you arrived?

TEMPLE: A porter helped us with the luggage, then Weston and his wife brought us upstairs.

STEVE: Paul, there's also Dr Steiner. He came in here after Weston and –

TEMPLE: By Timothy, yes! And he stood over by that chair for quite a while. But how could he possibly know –

FORBES: Steiner? Who exactly is this Dr Steiner?

TEMPLE: He is a Professor of Philosophy at Philadelphia University. We met him on board the Golden Clipper, coming over here from America.

FORBES: What's he doing in Scotland? Do you know?

TEMPLE: He's on holiday. As soon as he spotted our names in the hotel register he came up here …

TEMPLE pauses as he thinks of something.

FORBES: What's the matter?

TEMPLE: By Timothy! I'm a prize jackass if you like!

STEVE: Paul, what do you mean?

TEMPLE: Steve, don't you remember? I didn't sign a register. It was full. Weston made me sign on a sheet of notepaper. He put the paper in a drawer, so I don't see how Steiner could possibly have seen –

FORBES: Then he knew you were coming here. He was waiting for you – waiting for the letter!

TEMPLE: Just a minute. Not so fast, Sir Graham. It's not that simple …

42

STEVE:	Why should Dr Steiner, a respectable university professor, want that letter?
FORBES:	I presume you have only his word for his identity. What's his nationality?
TEMPLE:	Oh, obviously Austrian, I should say. Most probably Viennese.
FORBES:	Well, it seems a remarkable coincidence that he should be staying here the very night that Noel Hammond –
TEMPLE:	Who is this Noel Hammond? And who's this man van Draper? And who the devil is –
FORBES:	I can't tell you now, Temple. Come to my room after dinner – no, I'll come down here. It will be safer. We must get that letter back – no matter what happens we must get that letter! (*A pause*) I expect you'll be interested to know why I came to Scotland instead of going to the South of France.

SIR GRAHAM opens the door.

FORBES:	I'll see you both here, in about an hour.
TEMPLE:	Yes, all right.

SIR GRAHAM leaves and the door is closed.

STEVE:	Shall we go down to dinner now, Paul?
TEMPLE:	M'm? (*Suddenly*) Oh, excuse me, Steve, I wasn't listening. Darling, is there anything the matter?
STEVE:	No – nothing.
TEMPLE:	Come on, Steve, I know you better than that. You're worried about something, aren't you? You're upset about this business.
STEVE:	Yes. Yes, I am.

TEMPLE: Why?

STEVE: Well, so many things have started like this, haven't they? The Front Page Men, that awful business with the Knave of Diamonds, and –

TEMPLE: Darling, if you want to leave here first thing in the morning – we leave. You just have to say. And nothing on earth will stop us.

STEVE: You're very sweet.

The sound of the dinner gong is heard in the distance.

TEMPLE: I rather fancy that's for our benefit.

STEVE: Then it's certainly time for us to go and eat.

FADE SCENE.

FADE IN incidental music.

FADE incidental music.

FADE IN a door opening.

We are back in MRS MOFFAT's shop and the door bell sounds.

A second door opens.

MRS MOFFAT: What happened?

VAN DRAPER: (*Annoyed*) We missed him.

MRS MOFFAT: Missed him?

GUEST: It's no good beating about the bush, Draper. She'll have to know sooner or later.

MRS MOFFAT: Did something go wrong?

GUEST: We stopped the car and dished out a cock and bull story about Lindsay being out of his mind. They seemed to swallow it all right, but …

44

VAN DRAPER:	But instead of handing over the letter he presented us with these damned things.

VAN DRAPER shows MRS MOFFAT the packet of postcards.

MRS MOFFAT:	The postcards! That was canny of ye both, I must say.
VAN DRAPER:	(*Impatiently*) We can't stand here all evening, let's go upstairs.
MRS MOFFAT:	Why are ye both so anxious to get that letter? What was in it?
VAN DRAPER:	I've had my suspicions about Lindsay for a long time. Tonight they were –
MRS MOFFAT:	My God! You don't mean to say he's –
VAN DRAPER:	His name is not Lindsay at all, his name is Hammond – Noel Hammond. He's a British Agent. We ought to have checked up on him long ago, instead of accepting one person's word.
MRS MOFFAT:	But he was recommended by Z.2. She swore an oath that he could be trusted.
GUEST:	That little fool was taken in by him.
VAN DRAPER:	Z.2, that's Iris Archer, isn't it? She was liable to fall for that type. That's her one weakness. We should have realised that.
MRS MOFFAT:	You have always said that Lindsay was a good man at his job.
VAN DRAPER:	That's what Hardwick always assured me. Though just lately they don't seem to have been hitting it off too well.
GUEST:	That's all well and good but whatever happens we've got to get Lindsay.
VAN DRAPER:	That's imperative.
MRS MOFFAT:	Why is it so important?

VAN DRAPER:	Why? Good God, woman, don't you realise that Lindsay can blow up the whole bag of tricks? He's been working with Hardwick on the screen … he knows about us – about Z.4 –
MRS MOFFAT:	About Z.4? What exactly does he know about Z.4?
VAN DRAPER:	He knows that Z.4 is behind Hardwick. Also that Z.4 is at the head of the greatest espionage organisation in Europe.
MRS MOFFAT:	But does he know who Z.4 is?
GUEST:	Do any of us know that?
VAN DRAPER:	That's not the point. Lindsay or Hammond, whichever you like to call him, knows a great deal too much. There's Hardwick to start with …
GUEST:	And don't you believe me now that the British Intelligence know about Hardwick?
VAN DRAPER:	Of course they do. But fortunately for us they don't attach any importance to him – yet.
GUEST:	And after receiving Hammond's letter they might?
VAN DRAPER:	Precisely.
GUEST:	I wonder who this man … Richmond is?
VAN DRAPER:	Yes, so do I. I don't know – but if he's got that letter, there's nothing to do but to get him before he leaves.
MRS MOFFAT:	I shouldn't be surprised if Lindsay hasn't seen Richmond himself. In that case …
VAN DRAPER:	No. Lindsay won't be that stupid. He would keep clear of the village, I'm sure

of that. He'd reckon on us keeping an eye on The Royal Gate – that's why he didn't ask our friend for a lift.

GUEST: You know, I've got a hunch that Lindsay might return.

MRS MOFFAT: You mean – here?

GUEST: Yes, here.

MRS MOFFAT: Why should he?

GUEST: Well, in the first place he doesn't suspect that you happen to be one of us, and he'll probably be anxious to try and contact Richmond by telephone.

At that very moment the telephone rings.

MRS MOFFAT: Hello? … Yes … When did you arrive? … When? … I see. (*A pause. To GUEST, in a soft voice*) It's Z.2. (*Back into the phone*) Yes … Yes, I'm listening … Who? (*Very interested*) Paul Temple? … What does he look like? … Yes … yes –

VAN DRAPER: (*Whispering*) Ask her to come here. Maybe she knows something about Richmond.

MRS MOFFAT: (*Into the phone*) Listen, we need to see you … yes, straight away. Get here as soon as you can.

MRS MOFFAT replaces the receiver ending the call.

GUEST: So that was Z.2. I rather thought she was … on suspension.

VAN DRAPER: We needed her on this job. Z.4 ordered her to come up here.

MRS MOFFAT: Do ye know who that man was ... who gave ye the postcards?

VAN DRAPER: Not the faintest idea. Who was it?

47

MRS MOFFAT:	Paul Temple.
GUEST:	Paul Temple! My God, if Temple's on this job we can expect fireworks.
VAN DRAPER:	Paul Temple? What the devil is he doing here?
GUEST:	You don't suppose Temple happens to be Richmond, by any chance? That would account for his switching the postcards.
MRS MOFFAT:	Lindsay would have recognised him then.
GUEST:	Not necessarily. After all, none of us know who Z.4 is, but we take orders from him – or her.
VAN DRAPER:	We should hear something about Richmond from Z.2. If she's staying at The Royal Gate then obviously she must have seen Richmond.

In the background we hear the sound of the shop doorbell ring.

MRS MOFFAT:	Shhh!
VAN DRAPER:	Listen!
GUEST:	That's the shop door.
VAN DRAPER:	Who can it be at this time?
MRS MOFFAT:	I'll be right back.
VAN DRAPER:	Wait a minute.
MRS MOFFAT:	Well?
VAN DRAPER:	It might be Lindsay. If he wants to use the telephone – it's in order now. You understand?
MRS MOFFAT:	(*Sinisterly*) I understand.

MRS MOFFAT leaves and we hear her go down the stairs.
After a moment voices can be heard from below.

GUEST:	It's Hammond.

| VAN DRAPER: | Somehow or other, I thought he'd turn up. Right from the beginning I had a feeling we'd get him. Is your gun here? |
| GUEST: | If only Temple hadn't tricked us over that letter, we'd be sitting pretty now we've got Hammond. |

The sound of footsteps can be heard on the stairs.

| VAN DRAPER: | Sshh! |

The door opens and MRS MOFFAT and DAVID LINDSAY enter.

LINDSAY:	You never told me you had the phone connected up here.
VAN DRAPER:	Hello, Lindsay! Surprised?
LINDSAY:	Van Draper! Why, hello, I didn't expect –
GUEST:	Drop that gun!

A pause.

LINDSAY:	(*Softly*) What's the idea? What do you want from me?
GUEST:	There seems to have been a slight misunderstanding. Don't you agree, Mr Lindsay – or should I say Hammond?
LINDSAY:	Hammond? Who the devil is Hammond?
VAN DRAPER:	If you don't know … Your name is Hammond, Noel Hammond, employed by the British Intelligence Service.
LINDSAY:	British Intelligence? (*He laughs*) That's damned funny. If I'm from British Intelligence, why the devil do you think I worked with Hardwick? I've sweated my guts out on that blasted screen of his.
VAN DRAPER:	Oh yes. You worked very hard on the screen – we'll agree to that. But you had a reason.

LINDSAY:	Of course I had a reason. Six thousand reasons, to be exact.
MRS MOFFAT:	Six thousand? Did Z.4 promise you six thousand pounds if –?
LINDSAY:	No – dollars. I say, what the devil is all this about, anyway?
VAN DRAPER:	Two years ago, a certain Mr John Hardwick approached the War Office concerning an invention of his called the Hardwick Screen. This was tested and proved, to all intents and purposes, to be a failure –
LINDSAY:	And then I suppose the British Intelligence Department sent me along just in case?
VAN DRAPER:	Yes, just in case a certain other party became interested in the screen and any further developments.
LINDSAY:	I've never heard such damned nonsense in my life. If the War Office thought the screen was a washout, why should the Intelligence Department take an interest in the affair?
GUEST:	The answer to that is quite simple, my friend. They're after Z.4.
LINDSAY:	Very interesting, I'm sure.
VAN DRAPER:	The Intelligence Department discovered that Z.4 had contacted Hardwick, so they determined to kill two birds with one stone. (*Suddenly*) Keep away from that door!
LINDSAY:	Now listen to me, van Draper, put that revolver away and don't be a fool. Surely we can talk this over sensibly.

VAN DRAPER:	What was in that letter you sent to Richmond?
GUEST:	And who is John Richmond?
LINDSAY:	(*Nervously*) I – I haven't the faintest idea what you are talking about.
VAN DRAPER:	That's a pity, because I'm going to give you ten seconds to refresh your memory.

VAN DRAPER takes a watch from his pocket.

| VAN DRAPER: | Keep him covered, Guest. (*A pause*) Five … Six … Seven … Eight … Nine … Ten! |
| LINDSAY: | You – you can't do this! |

VAN DRAPER shoots and LINDSAY falls to the floor.

At just that moment the shop bell rings again.

| MRS MOFFAT: | That's the shop bell again. It's probably Z.2. |
| GUEST: | If it is Iris Archer, get her up here. |

The door opens as Mrs MOFFAT leaves.

| VAN DRAPER: | There's nothing special in his pockets. We'll have to get this body out of the way. Better get the car and heave him over Moorford Ridge. |

The door opens and MRS MOFFAT returns with IRIS ARCHER.

| IRIS: | Hello, Laurence. How long have you been up here? |

IRIS sees LINDSAY's dead body on the floor.

IRIS:	David!
GUEST:	Don't touch him!
VAN DRAPER:	I'm sorry – and particularly because Lindsay was a – friend of yours, but we have had to dispose of him.
IRIS:	But why?

A pause.

GUEST:	His name was Hammond. He was working for the Intelligence Service.
IRIS:	(*Astonished*) My God, I hope you don't think that I –
GUEST:	No. He had his tracks well covered.
IRIS:	Why, it's … it's unbelievable. I ran into Lindsay two years ago … he had a police record from here to Tokyo. I checked up on him before I even mentioned him to Z.4. Honestly, Laurence, I never even suspected –
VAN DRAPER:	That's all right. Hammond was a clever devil. He even convinced us that he was on the level.
GUEST:	When did you arrive?
IRIS:	Last night. How are things going?
GUEST:	Perfectly.
IRIS:	Is the screen ready yet?
GUEST:	Almost. We are waiting for Z.4.
IRIS:	You must mean you are waiting for instructions from Z.4.
MRS MOFFAT:	No.
VAN DRAPER:	We mean, we are waiting for Z.4 himself.
IRIS:	Don't be ridiculous! He's kept us in the dark so far, why should he –
VAN DRAPER:	This time Z.4 is coming out into the open.
IRIS:	When?
MRS MOFFAT:	Soon, very soon, we hope.
IRIS:	How do you know this?
GUEST:	Mrs Moffat had a letter almost two weeks ago. He's got four syndicates interested in the screen, and they are all

willing to pay over five million. The price may rise even higher – stimulated by competition. A million is neither here nor there to a government in the crazy armaments race.

IRIS: And how shall we know Z.4 when he arrives?

MRS MOFFAT: I'll know him by a quotation.

GUEST: Iris, there's a man staying at the inn called Richmond. John Richmond. Have you seen him?

IRIS: No, who is he?

GUEST: We have reason to suspect he's a British Agent. Lindsay sent him a letter, and we've got to know what was in it.

IRIS: A British Agent?

VAN DRAPER: What are you thinking about?

IRIS: I was just wondering if Paul Temple happened to be John Richmond.

GUEST: That's what I thought too.

VAN DRAPER: Get hold of Temple tonight. If necessary, go to his room.

GUEST: It might be a good idea to get Temple out of the way. Even if he doesn't happen to be Richmond, he's probably even more dangerous. I can't think he is merely up here for the good of his health.

VAN DRAPER: Yes. Yes, I think you're right.

IRIS: You mean … tonight?

VAN DRAPER: (*Quietly*) Tonight. As to the exact method, I leave that to you. Probably the situation will suggest something.

A pause.

IRIS:	Mrs Moffat, you said that you would recognise Z.4 by a quotation.
MRS MOFFAT:	Yes, I said that.
IRIS:	And the quotation is …?

A pause.

MRS MOFFAT:	What was it Shakespeare said – about travellers?

FADE SCENE.

FADE UP TEMPLE speaking.

TEMPLE:	I'm sorry, Sir Graham, but Steve has already been through quite enough for me in the past.
FORBES:	I can quite see your point of view, Temple, but I don't think you realise the seriousness of the situation.
TEMPLE:	I promised Steve we should leave here first thing in the morning, and I intend to keep my promise.

A pause.

FORBES:	(*Very seriously*) I'm sorry, Temple, but I'm afraid it's out of the question.
STEVE:	What do you mean?
FORBES:	(*Hesitantly*) Perhaps it might simplify matters if I told you something about this business. I can't tell you everything, Temple, for obvious reasons, but … well, I suppose I'd better start at the beginning, although where the devil the beginning is exactly, it's difficult to say. (*A pause*) About two years ago a man named John Hardwick got in touch with the War Office concerning an invention of his which he called the Hardwick

	Screen. Hardwick himself was a chemist who had inherited a large sum of money from some aunt or other.
TEMPLE:	What was this invention, exactly?
FORBES:	The Hardwick Screen was a system of camouflage for use on land, its chief advantage being –
STEVE:	You mean a smoke screen, similar to the sort of thing used by warships at sea?
FORBES:	Well, in a way, yes. But Hardwick's Screen differed from the kind of thing used by the Admiralty in several rather important details. However, that doesn't concern us at the moment.
TEMPLE:	Has Hardwick invented some kind of lamp or beam of some sort that could penetrate the screen?
FORBES:	That's just it, Temple, he had. And this is more or less where our story starts. The War Office gave the screen a try-out, and, to be brief, it was a terrible flop. The screen itself was all right, but the beam was a dismal failure. Without the beam, of course, the whole bag of tricks was a washout. Hardwick had the devil of a row with the War Office, and came back to Scotland.

FORBES pauses to relight his cigar.

FORBES:	After Hardwick had returned to Scotland, the Intelligence people began taking an interest in the matter.
STEVE:	You mean the Secret Service?
FORBES:	(*Laughing*) If you prefer that term, Steve. Yes, the Secret Service.

TEMPLE: But why should the Intelligence people be interested in the screen if the War Office had already turned it down?

FORBES: I'm glad you asked that question, Temple, because it's the crux of the whole matter. Do you mind if I have another cup of coffee, Steve?

STEVE pours out more coffee.

STEVE: There you are.

FORBES: Thank you.

TEMPLE: Go on, Sir Graham.

FORBES: For many years now, the British Intelligence Department, and Scotland Yard, too, for that matter, have realised that there existed in Europe one of the greatest independent espionage organisations of all time. An organisation under the direct control of one man – or woman. Someone under the pseudonym of Z.4.

TEMPLE: (*Softly*) Z.4?

STEVE: But what country do these people represent?

FORBES: They represent no country – and any country. They act according to the impulses of their personal selfishness and ...

TEMPLE: You mean these people trade in official secrets, irrespective of which country they are from?

FORBES: Yes. Now, after Hardwick had returned to Scotland, the British Intelligence had a hunch that Z.4 or one of his agents would contact him.

TEMPLE: But I don't understand. If the Hardwick Screen had already been proved a failure and the War Office had rejected it, why would Z.4 be interested in it?

STEVE: I've got it! You circulated a report that the test had been successful, knowing that under those circumstances Z.4 was almost bound to contact Hardwick.

FORBES: Steve, you're very clever. Roughly, yes, that was the idea.

TEMPLE: And a damned good idea, too.

FORBES: But we didn't let it rest there. A young man named Hammond, a brilliant research chemist and also a member of British Intelligence, had been interested in the Hardwick Screen from the very first. He was also interested – like everyone else in the Secret Service – in the identity of Z.4. Being a clever young devil, Hammond, or David Lindsay as he called himself, discovered that Iris Archer, your friend the actress, was a member of Z.4's organisation.

STEVE: Iris?

FORBES: He played up to her like blazes and before very long he found himself working side by side with her, and also directly in touch with Hardwick.

There is a knock on the door.

FORBES: What's that?

The knock is repeated.

STEVE: There is someone at the door, darling.

TEMPLE crosses, opens the door and looks out.

TEMPLE: There's nobody here.

FORBES: There's a note on the floor, Temple.

TEMPLE bends and picks up the letter.

TEMPLE: Good heavens...

FORBES: What is it?

TEMPLE:	It's the letter that Lindsay gave me. I recognise the envelope.
FORBES:	They don't seem to have opened it.
STEVE:	It seems strange that it should be returned like this – unopened.

FORBES tears open the envelope.

FORBES:	Listen to this! (*Reading*) Identity of Z.4 unknown even by important members of the organisation. Believe Z.4 to be in Scotland and likely to contact headquarters within the next three weeks. Have been compelled to work with Hardwick on behalf of Z.4. John Hardwick now prisoner at Skerry Lodge.
TEMPLE:	Looks like double-crossing.
FORBES:	My God, Temple! Listen to this! (*Reading*) Screen of definite value and importance. Beam almost perfected. Imperative Hardwick rescued. Contact Major Forster at once – N.H.
TEMPLE:	Screen of definite value – beam almost perfected.
FORBES:	I must get to a telephone immediately.

Before FORBES can go anywhere there is another knock on the door.

TEMPLE:	Come in.

The door opens and MRS WESTON enters.

TEMPLE:	Yes, Mrs Weston, what is it?
MRS WESTON:	Excuse me, sir, but Mrs Temple is wanted on the phone – from London.
STEVE:	I'm wanted on the telephone?
MRS WESTON:	That's right. They didn't say who it was.
TEMPLE:	But no one knows you're here, Steve.
STEVE:	No, no, of course not.

FORBES: That's damned funny, if you ask me. I'll come with you, Steve, then maybe I can get my call when you're finished.

STEVE: Yes, all right. Shan't be a minute, darling.

TEMPLE: Yes, all right, Steve.

STEVE, FORBES and MRS WESTON all leave and the door closes.

There is a pause whilst TEMPLE paces about the room humming to himself.

Suddenly the door opens again and IRIS ARCHER enters.

IRIS: May I come in?

TEMPLE: Why, Iris!

IRIS: Surprised?

TEMPLE: Well, it does seem a long way from the South of France.

IRIS: Are you going to ask me to sit down, or do I have to explain standing up?

TEMPLE: By all means …

IRIS: Where's Steve?

TEMPLE: She's downstairs taking a phone call. She won't be long. (*Pause*) What made you come to Scotland, Iris?

IRIS: Darling, I didn't know what to do. My doctor said I should go to Cornwall, I fancied the Riviera, so naturally –

TEMPLE: You struck a happy medium and came to Scotland.

IRIS: (*Laughing*) Exactly! Have you a light?

TEMPLE goes to the mantelpiece to get a box of matches.

IRIS: I'm so sorry, I never asked you to have a cigarette.

TEMPLE: Thank you.

TEMPLE takes a cigarette and lights both his and IRIS's.

IRIS: When did you arrive?

TEMPLE: About seven o'clock. And you?

IRIS: I came through yesterday, from Glasgow. Dreadful journey. It's the first time I've been to Scotland. I can't say I'm fond of it.

TEMPLE: It's really the wrong time of year, of course.

IRIS: Yes, darling, but it's so barren.

TEMPLE: There are worse places.

IRIS: How long are you staying here?

TEMPLE: We thought of leaving tomorrow morning.

IRIS: You're very wise. It's such awful weather, isn't it?

TEMPLE: Frightful.

A pause.

IRIS: Did you write to Seaman about the play?

TEMPLE: Yes, he was quite decent about it all.

IRIS: Oh, good. The play should stand a much better chance later in the year. Don't you think so?

TEMPLE: Probably.

IRIS: Temple, you know what I've come for, don't you?

TEMPLE: (*His voice becoming faint*) Yes, Iris, I know what you've come for.

IRIS: I want that letter, and I want it now.

TEMPLE: (*His voice even more faint*) Do you, Iris? (*A pause*) If the letter is of such … such … (*He appears to be having trouble speaking*)

IRIS: What's the matter?

TEMPLE: I – I don't know. My head – it's going round! My God, what have you done? There's a noise throbbing like – like –

TEMPLE falls against a chair.

IRIS: Feeling sleepy?

TEMPLE: What is it? What have you … done?

IRIS: (*Calmly*) The cigarette.

TEMPLE: The sig … The cigarette …

TEMPLE stumbles across the room and into the table. As he falls to the floor he brings the tea service down with him. There is an almighty crash.

IRIS: Right, there's no time to lose. I need to find that letter.

IRIS starts searching through TEMPLE's pockets.

IRIS: Watch, driving licence … what's this – insurance policy …

As IRIS continues to search she hasn't noticed that the door has opened again.

STEINER: You seem to be looking for something, madam. Can I be of any assistance?

IRIS: (*Turning suddenly; surprised*) Who the devil are you?

STEINER: Permit me to introduce myself. My name is Steiner. Dr Ludwig Steiner.

FADE IN closing music.

END OF EPISODE TWO

EPISODE THREE

INSTRUCTIONS
FOR A MURDER

OPEN TO:

IRIS: Right, there's no time to lose. I need to find that letter.

IRIS starts searching through TEMPLE's pockets.

IRIS: Watch, driving licence ... what's this – insurance policy ...

As IRIS continues to search she hasn't noticed that the door has opened again.

STEINER: You seem to be looking for something, madam. Can I be of any assistance?

IRIS: (*Turning suddenly; surprised*) Who the devil are you?

STEINER: Permit me to introduce myself. My name is Steiner. Dr Ludwig Steiner.

IRIS: What are you doing here? What do you want?

STEINER: I came to see Mr Temple, but it seems that my arrival is a little – premature.

IRIS dives into her handbag and produces a gun which she points at STEINER.

IRIS: (*Suddenly*) Get away from that door!

STEINER: I beg your pardon?

IRIS: (*Gruffly*) I told you to get away from that door.

STEINER: (*Rather nervously*) I trust that revolver is not loaded, madam.

IRIS: Unless you do as I say, you will have an opportunity of finding out.

STEINER: What is the matter with Mr Temple?

IRIS: He's not feeling so good. Now – get over into that corner.

STEINER: (*Bewildered*) But surely you –

IRIS: Get – over – in - the – corner!

STEINER: All right, if you insist ...

STEINER moves and IRIS resumes her search of TEMPLE's pockets.

IRIS: Nothing in his pockets.

STEINER: What is it you are looking for?

IRIS: What did you say your name was?

STEINER: Steiner, Dr Ludwig Steiner.

IRIS: Hmm … Is Temple a friend of yours?

STEINER: Madam, Mr Temple looks rather ill. I beg of you, let us –

IRIS: He's all yours, doctor. He's all yours.

IRIS leaves.

STEINER: Mr Temple! Mr Temple … what's the matter … what's wrong?

TEMPLE starts to regain consciousness.

TEMPLE: Oh, good heavens … my head feels terrible!

STEINER: No, don't try to get up … wait a moment.

TEMPLE: It's ok. Give me your hand.

STEINER: OK, but take it steady now.

STEINER helps TEMPLE up from the floor.

STEINER: There we are. Now sit in that chair for a moment.

TEMPLE: Has she gone?

STEINER: Yes, she's gone. Now stay where you are. I'll get you a cushion.

TEMPLE: I'll be all right in a minute.

STEINER: Perhaps a drink will help?

TEMPLE: No, thanks. (*He sighs*) I'm feeling a bit better already.

The door opens and STEVE returns with SIR GRAHAM.

STEVE: (*Startled*) Paul! Paul! What's the matter with you?

TEMPLE: It's nothing, dear.

FORBES: You look done in, Temple. What the devil has happened?

TEMPLE: After you left, Iris came here … she was looking for the letter … and …

FORBES: Take it easy, old man.

STEVE: This is Dr Steiner …

STEINER: I – I came here just to say hello, Mrs Temple. I was feeling a little lonely. When I opened the door, I saw that Mr Temple was ill, and that a strange woman –

FORBES: How long ago was this?

STEINER: But … just a moment ago.

FORBES: Wait here.

STEVE: It's no use.

FORBES: What do you mean?

STEVE: Iris has gone. Her car was outside before we went downstairs. Now it's disappeared. Look … you can see from the window. (*A pause*) Are you feeling any better, darling?

TEMPLE: Yes … I'm not so bad now.

FORBES: You were saying, Dr Steiner …?

STEINER: I found a strange woman searching Mr Temple's pockets. I did not know what to do – I was perplexed. Suddenly the lady in question produced a revolver, so I am afraid my actions became somewhat restricted, and alas – uninspired.

TEMPLE: I'm beginning to think it's a damned good job you turned up. That young lady meant business. She might have finished me off.

STEINER: (*Amazed*) But what was she actually doing here? What was she looking for?

FORBES: She was looking for a letter.

STEINER: A letter? It must have been a very important letter.

FORBES: Most important.

STEINER: Mrs Temple, I actually came here to ask if you and your husband would care to join me in a nightcap ... Perhaps under the circumstances, however ...

STEVE: Thank you, doctor, but I think perhaps it would be better if Paul went quietly to bed.

STEINER: Of course, of course! That goes without saying. Goodnight, Mr Temple. I hope we shall meet again before we leave ... (*To FORBES*) Goodnight, sir.

FORBES: Goodnight.

STEVE: Goodnight, doctor.

STEINER: Mrs Temple.

STEINER leaves and the door is closed.

TEMPLE: (*With a sigh of relief*) I'm feeling much better now.

STEVE: I think you should take it easy for a little while longer, dear.

TEMPLE: Yes, all right, Steve. By the way, who was that on the phone?

STEVE: That's exactly what I'd like to know. There was a woman at the other end ... she kept me waiting for ages, and then finally mumbled something about a wrong number. All the same, I'm pretty sure it wasn't a trunk call.

FORBES: The call was a fake – probably from a local box. They obviously wanted Steve out of the way while Iris did her stuff.

TEMPLE: Yes, that would be it. We should have guessed that. Sir Graham, did you get in touch with Major Forster?

FORBES: Yes, I got in touch with Forster all right.

TEMPLE: What's the matter?

FORBES: (*Grimly*) We're in a spot, Temple. A devil of a spot. And we need your help. I'm sorry, Steve, because I know how you feel, but things are serious – damn serious.

TEMPLE: What did Forster say?

FORBES: If Hardwick is on the right track – and according to Noel Hammond's report he most certainly is – then it's absolutely imperative that we get Hardwick away from Skerry Lodge.

TEMPLE: Yes, I agree with you.

STEVE: But surely Noel Hammond is at Skerry Lodge.

FORBES: Even if Hammond is alive, which I very much doubt, he's not likely to be at Skerry Lodge.

STEVE: I don't understand.

TEMPLE: Sir Graham means that since they know about the letter they must obviously know that Hammond – or David Lindsay as they call him – is a British Agent.

STEVE: Oh yes, I see that. But who exactly were those men who stopped us on the road?

FORBES: One was Laurence van Draper, and the other who called himself Lindsay was a gentleman by the name of Major Guest.

STEVE: Then you know these people?

FORBES: Oh yes, certainly. We know them all right. The Intelligence people know every member of the organisation, with the unfortunate exception of Z.4 … the one person who really matters.

STEVE: But if the Secret Service know these people, why on earth don't they do something about it?

FORBES: Well, for several reasons, Steve. You see, first of all you must realise that we are not up against a criminal organisation. These people are a vastly difference proposition from the

69

Front Page Men, for instance. Most of them are well educated, and to all intents and purposes, at any rate, thoroughly respectable. Take Iris Archer, for example – a well-known West End actress … Laurence van Draper – probably the most celebrated philatelist in Europe.

TEMPLE: I thought his name was familiar.

FORBES: Then there's Major Guest. He knows more about the Prenz machine gun than any man living.

STEVE: Yes, I've read about that, but if these people are so respectable, then –

FORBES: Just a minute, Steve, I didn't say they were respectable. I said – to all intents and purposes – they appear respectable. I think you will agree that there is a slight difference.

STEVE: All the same, if these people are so well known, there must be some reason why they are willing to risk their reputations and –

TEMPLE: Yes, that's true enough, Sir Graham. You said yourself that they represented no particular country, and since that seems automatically to wipe out any political factor …

FORBES: (*Quietly*) It doesn't rule out blackmail.

STEVE: Blackmail?

TEMPLE: What do you mean?

FORBES: Z.4 – whoever he or she may be – knows something incriminating about each member of the organisation. Of that I am sure.

TEMPLE: What makes you so sure of that?

FORBES: Do you remember Janet O'Donnell?

TEMPLE: You mean the Irish poet? Yes, definitely. She committed suicide, didn't she?

FORBES: Yes, she preferred suicide to being a member of Z.4's organisation.

STEVE: You mean that Z.4 was blackmailing –

FORBES: Exactly. But Z.4 isn't a fool. Make no mistake about that. The people are paid well. The blackmailing side of the business merely ensures their loyalty.

TEMPLE: I can't quite see why Hammond, or Lindsay, was working with Hardwick.

FORBES: Hammond was a research chemist. A very brilliant one, too. Z.4 obviously discovered this, and made use of the fact.

SIR GRAHAM returns to the letter and peruses it further.

FORBES: My God, I don't like the sound of this letter, Temple. (*Reading*) ...Screen of definite value and important ... beam almost perfected ... Whatever happens we must get Hardwick away from Skerry Lodge.

TEMPLE: Where exactly is this lodge?

FORBES: About four miles away – it's on the other side of High Moorford.

STEVE: Sir Graham, who do you think stole that letter?

FORBES: To tell the truth, I was inclined to think Dr Steiner – he seems a rum sort of bird. But if Steiner is a member of the organisation – or Z.4 himself for that matter – why should he return the letter?

There is a knock on the door.

STEVE: Come in.

MRS WESTON enters.

MRS WESTON:	Can I take the dirty coffee things?
STEVE:	I'm afraid we've had a bit of an accident – one of the cups is broken – I'm so sorry.
MRS WESTON:	That's all right, ma'am – these things do happen.

MRS WESTON gathers together the coffee things.

STEVE:	Would you like anything to drink, darling?
TEMPLE:	Yes, I think I'll have a brandy and soda. What about you?
FORBES:	Nothing for me.
MRS WESTON:	One brandy and soda, sir? I'll see to that for you. Shocking weather, isn't it?
STEVE:	(*Flippantly*) Does it always rain like this in Scotland?
MRS WESTON:	All the time I've been here – straight down and as wet as the devil. (*She giggles to herself*) I'll send your drink up right away, sir.
TEMPLE:	Thank you.

MRS WESTON leaves and the door is closed.

FORBES:	Temple, there's something I want to say to you. And it's not going to be easy. I don't quite know how to begin.
TEMPLE:	I think I know what it is, Sir Graham. But don't bother, we're leaving in the morning.
FORBES:	That's just the point, I don't want you to leave. Steve will have to go – that's imperative. But I need your help, Temple. I need it more than ever in my life before.
TEMPLE:	What do you mean?

FORBES: When I came up here, the Intelligence people
            told me my task would be a difficult one, and
            that I could use whatever means I thought fit,
            providing I succeeded. (*A pause*) I've got to get
            Z.4, Temple. No matter what happens, I've got
            to get Z.4!

TEMPLE: (*Softly*) And where exactly do I come in?

FORBES: Well ... you've met van Draper and Major
            Guest and –

TEMPLE: Isn't there another reason, Sir Graham?

FORBES: Yes. The people we are up against are now
            pretty certain that you are Richmond – the man
            Hammond's letter was intended for.

TEMPLE: M'm ... I'm not so sure about that yet.

STEVE: (*Quietly*) Sir Graham...

FORBES: Yes, Steve?

STEVE: Why do you want to get rid of me, Sir Graham?

FORBES: Things are too risky. In spite of their – what
            shall I call it? – veneer of respectability, these
            people are damnably dangerous.

TEMPLE: He's right, darling.

A pause.

STEVE: All right. You can run me over to Aberdeen in
            the morning. I believe there's a train at 12.10.
            I'll go down to Bramley Lodge for a few days.

TEMPLE: Yes – all right, Steve.

There is a knock on the door.

TEMPLE: Come in.

ERNIE WESTON enters.

ERNIE: One brandy and ginger ale, sir.

TEMPLE: I asked for a brandy and soda.

ERNIE: Oh – sorry, guv'nor, I'll go and –

TEMPLE: That's all right. Put it down here.

ERNIE: Yes, sir.

TEMPLE: Here, that's for you.

TEMPLE tips ERNIE.

ERNIE: Thank you, sir.

TEMPLE: Oh, by the way, Mr Weston, I lost a cigarette lighter this evening after dinner. I was wondering if you had seen it or not?

ERNIE: No, not me, guv'nor.

TEMPLE: It's rather a good one, and I should hate to lose it permanently.

ERNIE: I 'aven't seen no lighter – 'onest I 'aven't. I don't know if you think as 'ow there's any funny business goin' on 'ere, but –

TEMPLE: It's all right. I was just wondering, that's all. Goodnight.

ERNIE: Goodnight, sir. Goodnight. Goodnight, ma'am, sir.

STEVE: Goodnight.

ERNIE leaves and the door closes.

FORBES: Funny little devil. Nice to hear a bit of cockney, though, way up here.

STEVE: Darling, I didn't know you'd lost your lighter.

TEMPLE: I haven't.

STEVE: But then why did you –

TEMPLE: (*Laughing*) I just felt like it!

STEVE: (*Perplexed*) What?

There is a knock on the door.

TEMPLE: (*Softly*) Now who can that be?

There is a second knock on the door.

STEVE: Come in!

The door opens and REX BRYANT enters.

TEMPLE: Why, Bryant! What the devil are you doing here?

STEVE: Rex – this is a surprise!

BRYANT: Reporters do get about occasionally, you know. I once even went as far as Southampton to interview a novelist who had just landed on the Golden Clipper … but that's another story, as the subeditor said. Hello, Sir Graham, I didn't recognise you for a minute.

STEVE: This is Rex Bryant – Sir Graham Forbes.

FORBES: And what is Mr Bryant of the London Evening Post doing in Scotland?

BRYANT: Well, it's rather a long story. The editor got sarcastic – I got sarcastic. The editor got fresh – I got fresh. The editor got angry – I got –

STEVE: The sack?

BRYANT: Not exactly. In point of fact, I resigned. But it was a very close race; my tongue works a bit faster than his. I say, you look a bit off colour, Temple.

TEMPLE: I'm all right, Rex. But you still haven't told us why you've come to Scotland.

BRYANT: To see the bluebells, of course. Incidentally, I got a bit of a shock when I spotted your name in the register.

TEMPLE: In the register? Oh yes … Well, I think it might be a good idea if we all went downstairs and had a drink. What do you say?

BRYANT: Why not, Temple? Why not?

FADE SCENE.

FADE IN incidental music.

FADE music.

FADE IN MAJOR GUEST's voice.

GUEST: Any news of Iris?

VAN DRAPER: No. I feel like a drink. Ring for Ben.

GUEST rings a bell.

GUEST: I've been thinking, Van. Suppose Temple doesn't happen to be Richmond, and he's passed on that letter.

VAN DRAPER: Well, in that case it's all over, so far as the letter is concerned, at any rate.

GUEST: What do you think was in the letter?

VAN DRAPER: I don't know. Although we can be certain of one thing.

GUEST: What's that?

VAN DRAPER: Hammond discovered that Hardwick's beam wasn't such a washout after all. That meant, of course, that the screen could be of some use to the War Office. And consequently –

GUEST: Consequently the Intelligence people are going to swoop down on Skerry Lodge like – like – Well, anyhow, they're going to swoop down on us, and pretty soon too if you want my opinion.

VAN DRAPER: Assuming, of course, that the letter reaches Richmond.

GUEST: Yes, but even if it doesn't – or at any rate hasn't, we still have Temple to contend with.

VAN DRAPER: That rather depends, doesn't it, on whether or not Iris succeeded?

The door opens and BEN COLLINS enters.

BEN: Did you ring?

VAN DRAPER: Yes. Fetch me a whisky and soda.

BEN crosses to the sideboard and starts pouring the drink.

BEN: You haven't heard from Z.2 yet?

GUEST: No. We're expecting her at any minute.

BEN:	If she hasn't got that letter, we ought to get Hardwick and the screen out of here damn' quick, if you ask me.
GUEST:	Yes, that's what I say.
VAN DRAPER:	We can't do that. Not when we are expecting Z.4.
BEN:	Do you think that Z.4 really will come into the open this time?
VAN DRAPER:	He's got to.
GUEST:	But Hardwick's more or less finished working on the screen. We're all set – so what the devil is he waiting –
BEN:	Listen!

The door opens and IRIS enters.

VAN DRAPER:	Iris.
GUEST:	How did you get on?
IRIS:	Temple hasn't got the letter. What's more, he isn't Richmond.
GUEST:	Then who is?
IRIS:	I don't know.
VAN DRAPER:	What happened to Temple? Did you –
IRIS:	No. I used one of the cigarettes. It's no use putting him out of the way unless he intends to meddle.

The door opens suddenly and MRS MOFFAT enters.

VAN DRAPER:	Mrs Moffat – what is it?
GUEST:	You shouldn't have come here.
MRS MOFFAT:	I've had my instructions from Z.4.
VAN DRAPER:	What are they?

MRS MOFFAT reads from a note she is holding.

MRS MOFFAT:	(*Reading*) Paul Temple and his wife leave for Aberdeen tomorrow morning – by road.
GUEST:	Well?

MRS MOFFAT:	(*Reading*)They musn't reach Aberdeen alive. (*Finished reading*) That's all.
GUEST:	But how the devil can we stop them?
BEN:	There's a bridge, isn't there – not far from Skellyfore.
VAN DRAPER:	A bridge? What the devil has a bridge got to do with it?
BEN:	Have you ever been to Aberdeen by road from Inverdale?
VAN DRAPER:	No. I haven't.
BEN:	There's a bridge about two miles from a village called Skellyfore. Just over the bridge is a corner – Hell's Elbow, I think they call it. One of the worst corners you've ever come across. They've got a big "Danger" sign that hits you slap in the eye as you come to the bridge … Now if that "Danger" sign got lost somehow, and there was a car parked on the bend …
VAN DRAPER:	That's a damn' good idea!
GUEST:	Yes, but it might not be fatal.
BEN:	It would be fatal all right if there was something in the stationary car.
VAN DRAPER:	You mean – an explosive! So that when Temple's car hits the other … my God, Ben, that's an idea! That's certainly an idea!
IRIS:	Ben, I didn't think you'd got the brain.
VAN DRAPER:	I wonder how Z.4 knows that the Temples are planning to go to Aberdeen tomorrow.
GUEST:	The note seems to suggest that Z.4 must be staying at the inn, doesn't it?
VAN DRAPER:	Yes. That's true.
FADE SCENE.	

FADE IN incidental music.

FADE music.
FADE IN the sound of a car travelling at a fast speed.

STEVE: Paul, you're driving very fast.

TEMPLE: Sorry, darling, I'll slow down a bit.

STEVE: What was the name of that village we just drove through?

TEMPLE: Something with Skelly in it. Skellyfore, I think.

A pause.

STEVE: Paul …

TEMPLE: Yes, darling?

STEVE: You – you will take care of yourself, won't you?

TEMPLE: Of course I will. Good heavens, Steve, there's nothing for you to worry about.

STEVE: Why do you think Rex Bryant came to Inverdale?

TEMPLE: I haven't the faintest idea.

STEVE: His story about getting the sack didn't sound very convincing, did it?

TEMPLE: Oh, I don't know.

STEVE: Paul, I rather think Sir Graham suspects Dr Steiner.

TEMPLE: Dr Steiner … 'm …

STEVE: What exactly does that mean?

TEMPLE: Amongst other things, it means that Steiner was right about the hotel register.

STEVE: You mean that you did sign it after all?

TEMPLE: No. The landlord brought a new one out for the doctor to sign and added a few names from the old register – including ours.

STEVE: Then Dr Steiner really did see our names.

A car travelling behind the TEMPLEs' car toots its horn.

STEVE: Pull over, darling. There's a car wants to pass.

TEMPLE: He can't pass me here. It's much too narrow.
           Besides, there's a bridge ahead of us.

*The sound of the second car gets louder as it gets closer. Its
horn is still being sounded.*

STEVE: You'd better let him pass now before we get to
           the bridge.

TEMPLE: Don't be silly. Why should I?

STEVE: You'll have to let him pass at some point
           anyway, Paul.

TEMPLE: All right – anything to be rid of that dreadful
           horn. Come on – road hog!

The second car flies past the TEMPLE's car.

STEVE: I suppose he might be a doctor or something on
           the way to a serious case.

TEMPLE: He's certainly in a hurry to get somewhere.

A pause.

TEMPLE: My God! There's a corner on the other side of
           the bridge!

STEVE: Brake, Paul! Brake!

TEMPLE quickly applies the brakes on his car.

TEMPLE: He's going too fast! He's not going to be able
           to break in time.

STEVE: Oh, Paul!

*We hear the sound of a colossal collision, followed by a
terrible explosion.*

TEMPLE: Come along, Steve!

FADE SCENE.

FADE UP the sound of a burning car.

STEVE: Oh, Paul … the poor fellow … it's terrible.

TEMPLE: There's nothing we can do here to help, Steve.

STEVE: But who on earth left that car in such a position
           … and on this dreadful corner? It was madness!

TEMPLE: (*Calmly*) It was meant for us, Steve.

STEVE: For us? You mean we were meant –

TEMPLE: Come along, darling. We're going back to Inverdale.

FADE SCENE.

FADE IN the voice of SIR GRAHAM.

FORBES: Hello, Mrs Weston, is there something wrong?

MRS WESTON: Oh, it's you, Mr Richmond. I didn't hear you come in.

FORBES: Can I help at all?

MRS WESTON: It's … it's Ernie! He's … he's gone!

FORBES: Come on, Mrs Weston, pull yourself together! He'll show up all right. He's probably met some friends or –

MRS WESTON: But I can't understand it. He's never done anything like this before. We've been married for nigh on sixteen years and Ernie has never been away so much as an hour without telling me. He was never one for that sort of thing – always liked his home comforts and … and …

FORBES: When was the last time you saw your husband?

MRS WESTON: Last night. We'd locked up for the night, and was more or less getting ready for bed when Ernie suddenly said 'e'd take the dog for a walk. That was the last I ever …

MRS WESTON burst into tears.

STEINER: What seems to be the matter? Can I be of any help?

FORBES: It's Mr Weston.

STEINER: Our respected host? He is not ill, I trust?

81

FORBES: Not exactly. But – he's disappeared.

STEINER: Disappeared? But that is impossible. I saw him last night. Why, he served me with my lager just before supper.

FORBES: Yes, well, he hasn't been seen since.

STEINER: So?

REX BRYANT enters.

BRYANT: You wouldn't by any chance be talking about that little cockney bloke who was here when I arrived?

FORBES: Yes. Mrs Weston, when your husband went for a walk, did he seem in a good humour? He wasn't worried by any chance?

MRS WESTON: Er – no – I don't think so.

FORBES: What time was it exactly – do you remember?

MRS WESTON: Well, as near as I can tell, about eleven.

BRYANT: You mean this fellow went out at eleven last night and hasn't been seen since?

FORBES: How was he dressed?

MRS WESTON: He had his blue serge trousers on – and an old sports jacket – and, I believe, a white muffler.

The door opens and TEMPLE and STEVE enter.

FORBES: Hello, Temple. Why, hello, Steve – I thought –

TEMPLE: I want to see you straight away – come to my room. Could I have the key, Mrs Weston? Number 172.

MRS WESTON: So you decided not to leave us after all, eh, Mrs Temple? That is good.

STEVE: Is anything the matter, Mrs Weston?

FORBES: Mrs Weston is very upset.

TEMPLE:	Why? What's the trouble?
FORBES:	Weston went out last night about eleven o'clock – and he hasn't been seen since.
STEVE:	You mean he's – disappeared?
FORBES:	Yes. It looks like it.
TEMPLE:	Oh, but that's impossible! Don't worry, Mrs Weston. He'll turn up all right.
MRS WESTON:	Thank you, sir. Here's your key.
TEMPLE:	Thank you. Coming, Steve?
FORBES:	Let me carry that case, Steve.
STEINER:	We shall see you both later, I hope?
STEVE:	Why, yes, of course, doctor.
BRYANT:	I'd like a word with you, Temple, if I may.
TEMPLE:	Yes, all right. Come to my room in about ten minutes.

FADE SCENE.

FADE IN STEVE's voice.

STEVE:	Put the case down anywhere, Sir Graham.
FORBES:	Temple, what on earth made you change your mind about going to Aberdeen? It must have been something –
TEMPLE:	Have you ever heard of Hell's Elbow, Sir Graham?
FORBES:	Why, yes, it's that very bad corner about two miles from Skellyfore, isn't it?
TEMPLE:	Yes. Well, someone parked a car on the corner – and if a poor devil in a sports car hadn't tried to show off and …
STEVE:	Look at the cupboard!
TEMPLE:	What's the matter with it?
STEVE:	I mean … on the floor … there's some red paint or ink or something … it looks as if …

83

TEMPLE: That's not paint.

FORBES: We'd better open the door, Temple.

FORBES tries opening the door but it is locked.

FORBES: That's damn' queer. We'll have to force it open, that's all.

TEMPLE: Allow me. This pocket-knife usually does the trick.

After a few moments of maneuvering TEMPLE manages to open the wardrobe door. ERNIE WESTON's body falls out of it.

FORBES: What the –?

STEVE: Paul, it's Ernie Weston!

FORBES: Temple, is he –?

TEMPLE: Yes. He's dead all right. Almost instantaneous I should think.

STEVE: Oh, Paul, how horrible … how horrible!

FORBES: Look out, Temple, she's going to faint!

TEMPLE: It's ok, Steve, I've got you!

STEVE: I'm – I'm all right.

TEMPLE: Yes, but I think you'd better sit down for a moment.

STEVE: Yes. Yes, all right, darling.

TEMPLE: There we are. (*A pause*) Anything on the body, Sir Graham?

FORBES: There's something in his hand. It looks to me like a watch chain.

TEMPLE: Let me see. Yes, it's a watch chain all right. I've seen it before somewhere, too.

FORBES: Now you come to mention it, I think I've seen something like it.

STEVE: That watch chain. I know whose it is!

TEMPLE: Steve, do calm yourself, darling.

STEVE: But I know that chain – I've often noticed it.

FORBES: Oh! Who does it belong to?

84

STEVE: It belongs to Rex Bryant.
TEMPLE: Rex Bryant?
FADE IN closing music.

END OF EPISODE THREE

EPISODE FOUR

APPOINTMENT
WITH DANGER

OPEN TO:

FORBES: Look out, Temple, she's going to faint!

TEMPLE: It's ok, Steve, I've got you!

STEVE: I'm – I'm all right.

TEMPLE: Yes, but I think you'd better sit down for a moment.

STEVE: Yes. Yes, all right, darling.

TEMPLE: There we are. (*A pause*) Anything on the body, Sir Graham?

FORBES: There's something in his hand. It looks to me like a watch chain.

TEMPLE: Let me see. Yes, it's a watch chain all right. I've seen it before somewhere, too.

FORBES: Now you come to mention it, I think I've seen something like it.

STEVE: That watch chain. I know whose it is!

TEMPLE: Steve, do calm yourself, darling.

STEVE: But I know that chain – I've often noticed it.

FORBES: Oh! Who does it belong to?

STEVE: It belongs to Rex Bryant.

TEMPLE: Rex Bryant?

FORBES: She's right, Temple! When he arrived here last night I remember seeing him wear it.

TEMPLE: (*Pondering*) Yes. Nothing much else here. Hello, what's this?

FORBES: It looks like a wedding ring.

TEMPLE: (*As if in thought*) Yes.

STEVE: It looks like rather an expensive one too.

FORBES: Now what the devil would Ernie Weston be doing with a platinum wedding ring?

TEMPLE: (*Softly*) H'm … this rather bears out what I thought.

STEVE: Sir Graham, you don't think Ernie Weston has anything to do with this other business, do you?

FORBES: (*In thought*) I don't know, Steve. I have to admit at the moment I don't know what to think.

There is a knock on the door.

STEVE: That's probably Rex Bryant now. Remember, he wanted to speak to you, Paul.

TEMPLE: Yes.

FORBES: Let him come in, Temple.

STEVE: Come in, Rex.

The door opens and REX BRYANT enters.

BRYANT: (*Good-humoured*) Sorry to barge in like this, old man. Oh, I say, is there something wrong? (*A pause*) Oh my goodness!

FORBES: It's Ernie Weston.

BRYANT: My God! Is he dead?

FORBES: Yes, he's dead.

BRYANT: But what happened? Where did he come from? Damn it all, don't stand there staring at me as if – Just a minute, where did you get that watch chain?

FORBES: You've seen it before?

BRYANT: Why, of course I've seen it before. It's mine.

STEVE: You don't deny it?

BRYANT: Deny it? Of course I don't deny it. Why the devil should I?

TEMPLE: When we found Weston, he had that watch chain in his hand.

BRYANT: In his hand?

TEMPLE: It rather looked as if there had been some sort of struggle.

BRYANT: (*Somewhat startled*) My God, Temple, you don't think I had anything to do with this?

TEMPLE: The watch chain, Rex, is evidence – rather important evidence, I should say.

BRYANT: I don't know whether this is some sort of joke, Temple! Good God, man, why should I kill Weston? I'd never even met the fellow before – before I came here.

FORBES: And what about the watch chain? How do you account for that?

BRYANT: I – I lost it. Last night after I got to bed I noticed it wasn't in my waistcoat.

FORBES: Did you mention this to anyone?

BRYANT: No. I thought it had slipped out – the fastening was loose – they do sometimes. Wait a minute! Yes, I did – I mentioned it to Dr Steiner. He was telling me about some gold cufflinks he'd lost, and we were wondering –

TEMPLE: You were wondering what?

BRYANT: Well, as a matter of fact we thought the cufflinks and watch chain might have – got together.

STEVE: You mean, you thought perhaps they'd both been stolen by the same person?

BRYANT: Yes, and you can take it from me, Temple –

TEMPLE: I have my own ideas about this business, Rex. But I should like you to tell us why you came to Scotland in the first place.

BRYANT: (Slowly) Why I came to Scotland?

TEMPLE: Yes.

A pause.

BRYANT: I came to Scotland because of a man named Hardwick – John Hardwick.

FORBES: Hardwick! What the devil do you know about Hardwick?

TEMPLE: Well, Rex?

BRYANT: About a week ago, Sir Graham, a man walked
           into the offices of the Evening Post. He was an
           untidy-looking individual, but in spite of his
           clothes he had a certain – what shall I say? – a
           certain "air" about him. He asked to see the
           news editor, but Cosgrove was in one of his
           "touch-me-not" moods, and he sent me out to
           have a chat with the fellow. He likes to unload
           that sort of job on me. Why, I could tell you
           things about Cosgrove that –

FORBES: All right, all right – go on with your story!

BRYANT: Well, as it happened, on this occasion the
           fellow told me a damned interesting story. First
           of all, he said his name was Hardwick – Hubert
           C. Hardwick, and that his brother, John
           Hardwick, had invented some sort of a smoke
           screen which, coupled with an invention known
           as the Inverdale Beam, would set the War
           Office all agog. Now I'd already heard of John
           Hardwick, and I knew for a fact that the War
           Office had turned down the invention because
           the Inverdale Beam had proved to be a failure.

TEMPLE: Did Hubert Hardwick know this?

BRYANT: He did. But this is the extraordinary part about
           the business. Apparently, after the invention
           had been rejected, John Hardwick returned to
           Inverdale, and started work all over again on
           the beam. About two or three months later his
           brother – the chappie I saw – tried to get in
           touch with him, and rather to his surprise was
           unable to do so. He came up to Inverdale for
           two or three weeks in the hope of staying for a
           short while at Skerry Lodge, but he couldn't

even get farther than the main gate. So, in desperation, he returned to London.

FORBES: Is this Hubert C. Hardwick a wealthy man?

BRYANT: Just the opposite. He hasn't got a bean.

FORBES: Go on.

BRYANT: Well, there's very little more to tell, really. Hubert Hardwick was convinced that his brother was being held a prisoner and was hoping that we'd take the trouble to investigate the matter and pay him a pretty substantial fee for the privilege of doing so. The poor devil didn't know much about Fleet Street, I'm afraid.

STEVE: What did Cosgrove say to all this?

BRYANT: You know Cosgrove as well as I do, Steve. I think he had some sort of idea that I'd made it all up. I tried to convince him that the story was well worth a break, but he wouldn't even listen. About two weeks later I got the sack. To be quite honest, Temple, it was the day after I saw you at Southampton. Naturally, I felt pretty despondent about things – I'd been on the London Evening Post for nearly ten years – and between me and you I made a pretty good attempt to liquidate my sorrows, as it were. Late that night, and purely by chance, I ran into Hubert C. Hardwick. I was pretty well sozzled by the time we met, and for the first couple of hours I don't believe I even realised who the devil he was. Anyhow, he'd been up to Inverdale since our first meeting, but he'd met with very little success. Skerry Lodge was guarded like Woolwich Arsenal. It was utterly impossible to get near the place. Well, to be brief, I got pretty curious. It seemed to me that a first-rate scoop was just sitting up waiting to be –

FORBES: And so you came to Scotland.

BRYANT: Exactly, Sir Graham.

TEMPLE: Have you been near Skerry Lodge since you arrived?

BRYANT: You bet your life.

TEMPLE: What sort of place is it?

BRYANT: It looks more like a medieval castle than anything else. It's built on the side of a small lake in the hills – Loch Abafford I believe they call it.

TEMPLE: Did you get near the house?

BRYANT: As a matter of fact, I didn't try. Hubert Hardwick's frontal attack had failed, so I decided to get the lie of the land before I did any real sightseeing.

STEVE: (*Quietly*) Paul, don't you think one of us ought to see Mrs Weston and …?

TEMPLE: Yes, I've been thinking about that too, Steve. I think it might be a good idea if you broke the news. You seem to be able to handle her better than we do.

STEVE: Yes, all right. I'll go and see her. Oh dear, she is going to be very upset.

The door opens, STEVE leaves, and the door closes.

FORBES: Here's your watch chain, Bryant. I should take better care of it in future.

BRYANT: Look here, Sir Graham, I don't know whether you still think I had anything to do with this business, but I can assure you on my word of honour that –

TEMPLE: Have you seen this before?

94

BRYANT: Why, no. What is it? Looks like a wedding ring.

TEMPLE: Yes. I should imagine that's what it is.

BRYANT: Where did you get it?

TEMPLE: We found it – on Weston.

BRYANT: No, I've definitely not seen it before.

TEMPLE: What was it you wanted to see me about?

BRYANT: I think we'll leave that till later. It's not very important …

TEMPLE: OK. Then you might pop downstairs and see how Steve's getting on with Mrs Weston – she might want some help. I'm afraid it'll be a dreadful shock for the old girl.

BRYANT: All right.

The door opens, BRYANT leaves and the door closes.

FORBES: This business is getting serious, Temple – damned serious. We've got to get Hardwick away from Skerry Lodge – and above all we've got to get Z.4.

TEMPLE: If John Hardwick has succeeded in perfecting the Inverdale Beam he'll have served his purpose – so far as Z.4 is concerned, at any rate.

FORBES: Yes, but according to the letter we received from Lindsay, or rather Hammond, he hasn't perfected it. At least, not quite. We may still be in time, Temple.

TEMPLE: Have you got that letter, Sir Graham?

FORBES: Yes.

TEMPLE: (*Reading*) Identity of Z.4 unknown even by important members of organisation. Believe Z.4 to be in Scotland and likely to contact headquarters within next three weeks.

FORBES: Headquarters. I wonder if Hammond meant Skerry Lodge.

TEMPLE: I don't know. If the identity of Z.4 is unknown then how will he contact the organisation? They must have some means of identification, or –

FORBES: Z.4 has probably supplied them with some sort of passwords so that when he does contact them they will instantly recognise him – or her.

TEMPLE: You don't think Iris Archer happens to be Z.4?

FORBES: I don't know, Temple.

TEMPLE: (*Quietly*) Rather like a medieval castle ... that's what Bryant said about Skerry Lodge, isn't it?

FORBES: Yes.

TEMPLE: Sounds interesting. I think it might be quite a good idea if Steve and I drove over there.

FORBES: For God's sake don't take any risks. (*A pause*) Temple.

TEMPLE: Yes.

FORBES: Who do you think murdered Weston?

TEMPLE: Z.4.

FORBES: But – why?

TEMPLE: Exactly, Sir Graham. But – why?

FORBES: Do you think Ernie Weston was a member of the organisation?

TEMPLE: I'm almost sure he wasn't.

There is a knock on the door.

It opens and DR STEINER enters.

STEINER: May I come in, Mr Temple?

TEMPLE: Dr Steiner! Why, yes, please do.

STEINER: This is a dreadful business, is it not? I have just left Mrs Temple, she told me about ... about this poor fellow.

TEMPLE: Dr Steiner, is it true that you lost a pair of cufflinks the night you arrived here?

STEINER: (*Surprised*) Why, yes – yes, that's true. But why do you ask? Perhaps they have been found – yes?

TEMPLE: No. I'm afraid they haven't. But I think you'll get them back all right.

STEINER: I hope so. I sincerely hope so.

FORBES: Dr Steiner, I wonder if you would permit me to ask you a rather unusual question?

A slight pause.

STEINER: But – of course. Go ahead.

FORBES: What are you doing in Scotland?

STEINER: In Scotland? Why … I am on holiday.

TEMPLE: Perhaps it would be just as well if I introduced –

FORBES: My name is Richmond. John Richmond.

STEINER: And mine, sir, is Steiner – Doctor Ludwig Steiner, Professor of Philosophy at the University of Philadelphia.

FADE SCENE.
FADE IN incidental music.

FADE music.
FADE IN the voice of VAN DRAPER.

VAN DRAPER: (*Irritated*) But my goodness, you saw the car, Guest. Why the devil didn't you make some attempt to stop it?

GUEST: Stop it? Don't talk such damned nonsense. The idiot must have been doing at least sixty miles an hour!

BEN: (*Irritated*) All right, all right. There's no need to start going into that all over again.

VAN DRAPER: What's that?

97

The door opens and IRIS enters.

IRIS: Not the slightest need.

GUEST: Oh, so you're back. What's happened about Temple?

IRIS: He's back at the inn.

IRIS pours herself a drink.

IRIS: The car idea wasn't so hot after all, eh, Ben?

BEN: Everything would have been fine if only that damned fool of a driver hadn't stepped on the accelerator and got there first.

IRIS: What happened to that man? Did he get out ok?

BEN: (*Quietly*) He got what Temple was meant to get.

GUEST: I'm beginning to think Temple is one of those lucky devils who can't be put out of action.

VAN DRAPER: If Temple is still at the inn, you'd better take care of him, Iris.

IRIS: That's out of the question. I can't go back there – not now.

GUEST: Of course she can't, Laurence.

VAN DRAPER: Temple has got to be taken care of. We've bungled one attempt, and we mustn't bungle another.

MRS MOFFAT: Indeed we mustn't.

VAN DRAPER: Mrs Moffat!

MRS MOFFAT closes the door.

GUEST: What are you doing here?

MRS MOFFAT: You've got to get Hardwick away.

VAN DRAPER: Why?

GUEST: What has happened?

BEN: My God! Don't say the police –

IRIS:	You've had instructions from Z.4?
MRS MOFFAT:	Yes. (*Pause*) But there's nothing to get alarmed about, only we've got to get Hardwick and the screen away from Skerry Lodge.
VAN DRAPER:	(*Softly*) But – why?
MRS MOFFAT:	Because of Temple.
VAN DRAPER:	I don't understand.
MRS MOFFAT:	Paul Temple is coming here.
GUEST:	Here?
VAN DRAPER:	How do you know that?
MRS MOFFAT:	Instructions from Z.4.
BEN:	And what's going to happen?
MRS MOFFAT:	Van Draper and Guest can take Hardwick down to the chalet. You must hold him there until you receive word from Ben.
BEN:	And what am I supposed to be doing while all this is going on?
MRS MOFFAT:	You will be entertaining Mr Temple.
BEN:	Entertaining Temple!
MRS MOFFAT:	When Temple arrives you will show him in here, and then go down into the basement.
VAN DRAPER:	The basement?
BEN:	My God! You don't want me to flood the basement?
MRS MOFFAT:	That is exactly what I do want you to do! Only make certain that Temple is in the basement before the water reaches the first grid.
GUEST:	Why, he'll be trapped like a rat!
BEN:	The idea's all right, if we can only get Temple into the basement.
MRS MOFFAT:	You'll get him there, if you use your head.

BEN: (*Absently, in thought*) Yes... Yes...

VAN DRAPER: (*Suddenly*) We'd better start packing the
                screen apparatus.

BEN: Just a minute! What the devil happens to
                me after it's all over?

MRS MOFFAT: You'll meet Iris at the junction near High
                Moorford. She'll bring you down to the
                chalet. Is that clear, Iris?

IRIS: It looks as if I won't get that part in
                Temple's new play after all.

BEN: You'd better give me a hand with that
                pump. It takes a devil of a time to get it
                going.

GUEST: All right.

IRIS: (*Brusquely*) I'm off now. I'll see you later,
                Ben.

BEN: O.K. And for God's sake mind you're
                there in time.

MRS MOFFAT: I don't think Hardwick will give you any
                trouble, but if he does, you'll know what
                to do.

VAN DRAPER: Don't worry about Hardwick. We'll
                handle him all right.

GUEST: I can't see why the devil we should take
                Hardwick down to the chalet – just
                because of Temple. If we intend to get
                Temple, then why on earth don't we –

MRS MOFFAT: We can't take any chances. Not where
                Paul Temple is concerned.

GUEST: H'm, perhaps you're right.

IRIS: Shall you come down to the chalet, Mrs
                Moffat?

MRS MOFFAT: I can't – because of Z.4. I may be wanted.

FADE SCENE.

FADE IN incidental music.

FADE music.

FADE IN the sound of footsteps on a gravel path.

TEMPLE: By Timothy, Bryant was certainly right about this place.

STEVE: (*Nervously*) Darling, don't you think we ought to go round to the side of the house before we try the front?

TEMPLE rings the doorbell.

TEMPLE: Too late I'm afraid, my darling.

STEVE: Oh, Paul!

TEMPLE: Now it's perfectly all right, Steve. Don't get frightened.

A pause.

STEVE: Can you hear anything?

TEMPLE: Sh! There's someone coming.

The door opens.

BEN: (*In his finest voice*) Good evening, sir

TEMPLE: Good evening. I should like to see Mr Hardwick. My name is –

BEN: Mr Hardwick is very busy at the moment, sir, but if you'll be so good as to step this way.

TEMPLE: Thank you. Come along, Steve.

The door is closed.

There is a pause.

An inner door opens.

BEN: What name shall I say, sir?

TEMPLE: Temple … Paul Temple.

BEN: Certainly, sir, just a moment, sir.

BEN leaves and the door is closed.

STEVE: (*Ill at ease*) Paul, we shouldn't have come here.

TEMPLE: (*Quietly*) It's all right, darling. There's nothing to be afraid of.

TEMPLE attentively takes in the surroundings of the room.

TEMPLE: I say, it's a pretty decent sort of house, this …
Certainly believes in doing himself well …
There's certainly been some sort of a party here
– look at all these cigarette butts in the ashtray.

STEVE: I didn't notice Sir Graham when he left the inn.
I hope you told him that we were coming here.

TEMPLE: Sir Graham was telephoning – something rather
important, I should imagine. (*Suddenly*)
Hardwick must be worth a packet by the look
of things. Just take a look at this picture!

Footsteps can be heard in the distance.

STEVE: What is it?

TEMPLE: He's coming back!

The door opens and BEN enters.

BEN: Mr Hardwick is extremely busy, sir, but if
you'd care to step down to the laboratory, I
think he might be able to spare you a few
moments.

TEMPLE: Yes, of course. Come along, Steve.

BEN: I should leave your things here, sir. You'll be
able to pick them up on the way back.

TEMPLE: Very well. Thank you.

FADE SCENE.

FADE IN BEN's voice.

Footsteps can be heard coming down some stairs.

BEN: This way, sir … this way, madam

*BEN opens a door and TEMPLE and STEVE follow him into
another room.*

BEN: Mr Hardwick will be along directly.

TEMPLE: Thank you.

BEN leaves and closes the door.

STEVE: Paul – I don't like the look of this place.

TEMPLE: No, I'm not exactly enamoured myself.

TEMPLE walks over and tries the handle.

STEVE: Paul – what is it?

TEMPLE: He's locked us in.

TEMPLE struggles with the door handle for a moment or two.

TEMPLE: My God, Steve, we ought to have had more sense!

STEVE: But – why have they done this? I don't understand –

TEMPLE: For precisely the same reason that they left the car on Hell's Elbow. Obviously, our visit wasn't the surprise I thought it would be.

STEVE: Couldn't we break the door down?

TEMPLE: Not this door, I'm afraid.

STEVE: Paul, look! Why is it padded at the foot?

TEMPLE: I don't know.

STEVE: What is it?

TEMPLE: I thought I heard something.

STEVE: Paul – look! Look at that ventilator! There's water coming through it!

TEMPLE: Good grief. So that's it.

STEVE: They're – they're flooding the room!

Water can clearly be heard flowing into the room now.

TEMPLE: Open this door!

TEMPLE starts hammering on the door.

TEMPLE: Open this door, I say!

STEVE: Oh, Paul, we've got to get out of here somehow!

TEMPLE: Open up I tell you – let us out!

STEVE: Oh, darling …

TEMPLE: It's no use, I'm afraid. We'll just have to wait and see what happens.

Water continues to flow into the room.

TEMPLE: Frightened, dear?

STEVE: Yes, I am rather. I don't mind admitting it.

TEMPLE: At this rate, I should say we've got about an hour. Possibly longer – it's difficult to tell.

STEVE shivers.

TEMPLE: Cold?

STEVE: (*Very scared*) Yes.

TEMPLE: Steve.

STEVE: Yes, darling.

TEMPLE: I'm – I'm terribly sorry about this business. That we've ended up like this. I should have listened to you better.

STEVE: Don't be silly, Paul. It … it just can't be helped … that's all. We'll just have to face it together.

TEMPLE: There's nothing we can do, I'm afraid, except wait.

STEVE: I suppose this room is on the side of the lake.

TEMPLE: Yes, it must be. (*A pause*) It's funny … I've often wondered how people under these sort of circumstances would react … I actually always thought … (*Suddenly*) What is it, dear?

STEVE: Nothing. I was just thinking – that's all.

TEMPLE: Thinking?

STEVE: Do you remember that first summer, darling?

TEMPLE: When we went to Capri?

STEVE: Yes – Capri. The blue sky … the gay little houses … the crazy little steamer … and the donkey.

TEMPLE: Ah yes, the donkey. A stubborn fellow at the best of times. (*A pause*) I'm so sorry I landed you in this mess, darling.

STEVE: It's … nothing.

TEMPLE suddenly jumps up.

TEMPLE: Good God! We're talking as if the whole business were over and we were finished! We got ourselves into this, and we're going to get ourselves out of it!

TEMPLE bangs on the door again.

TEMPLE: Hello! Is anyone there?!!

STEVE: It's no use, Paul. What can we do?

TEMPLE: Hello!!! Is anyone there?!!! (*Pondering*)I'm afraid the door is hopeless. But we might be able to stop the water, though.

TEMPLE takes off his coat.

TEMPLE: Hold my coat for a moment, Steve.

STEVE: What are you going to do?

TEMPLE: Try to stop the water from coming in, of course. If I could just manage to close one of those grates ... Here, hand me my coat, darling. If I can just manage to block this one ...

STEVE: But what about the other one?

TEMPLE struggles to block one of the grates with his coat thus restricting the flow of water.

TEMPLE: If I can at least block this one then we can last a bit longer. (*A pause*) There, that's done it.

STEVE: (*Suddenly*) Paul!

TEMPLE: What is it?

STEVE: Didn't you hear anything?

TEMPLE: (*Listening*) No ... and I don't think my coat is going to last for very long, I'm afraid.

STEVE: Paul – listen!

FORBES: (*Calling from outside*) Temple! Temple! Where are you? Temple! Can you hear me?!

TEMPLE: My God! It's Sir Graham! We've got to make him hear us, Steve! Sir Graham! Sir Graham, we're here!

STEVE: We're here!

TEMPLE starts banging on the door again as he continues to shout out.

STEVE: We'll have to be quick – the water's pouring in fast again!

TEMPLE: Sir Graham! Sir Graham! Quickly, give me that chair, Steve!

STEVE: What are you going to do?

TEMPLE: Look! There's a fanlight above the door! It's so dirty I didn't notice it before … If I can just smash it, Sir Graham might be able to hear us better.

STEVE: Good luck!

TEMPLE smashes the chair against the fanlight and there is a crashing of glass.

STEVE: Oh, you've cut yourself, darling.

TEMPLE: No, it's nothing. I'm all right. Sir Graham! Sir Graham!

FORBES: (*Outside*) Where the devil are you, Temple?

TEMPLE: We're at the end of the corridor. For God's sake, be quick!

Footsteps can be heard running towards the room.

FORBES: Stand back from the door!

TEMPLE: Stand back, Steve!

Several heavy blows on the door can be heard from the other side. Eventually, a panel of the door gives way.

FORBES: Temple! There you are!

STEVE: Oh, Sir Graham, thank goodness!

FORBES: Now stand back whilst I break this damned lock.

SIR GRAHAM deals a heavy blow to the lock and it breaks and the door bursts open. As it does so water floods out of the room covering SIR GRAHAM's feet.

FORBES: What the –? I say, Temple, what's been going on here?

TEMPLE:	We'll explain later. Let's just get out of here.
FORBES:	Yes, all right, come on.
TEMPLE:	Did you get any of them?
FORBES:	Yes. We arrested Ben Collins and Iris Archer.
TEMPLE:	Iris?
FORBES:	Yes, she was in a car at the High Moorford junction – obviously waiting to pick Collins up.
TEMPLE:	Come on, Sir Graham – let's get back.

FADE SCENE.
FADE IN incidental music.

FADE music.
FADE IN IRIS's voice.

IRIS:	Really, Paul, I can't for the life of me think what this is all about.
TEMPLE:	(*Quietly*) Sit down, Iris.
IRIS:	But I haven't done anything.
BEN:	You've got nothing on me! I don't know anything – about anything.
TEMPLE:	Where did they take Hardwick?
BEN:	I don't know. (*Angrily*) I don't know what the 'ell all this is about!
TEMPLE:	You soon will, my friend.
FORBES:	Where have they taken Hardwick?
BEN:	For God's sake don't keep on asking me the same ruddy questions!

Suddenly the door opens and DR STEINER and REX BRYANT enter.

STEINER:	I am given to understand that you want to see me, Mr Temple.
TEMPLE:	Ah, doctor! And you too, Rex. Come in!
BRYANT:	I hope I'm not intruding. But Steve said that you wanted a word with me.

FORBES: Dr Steiner, is this the young lady who was with Mr Temple when –

STEINER: Why, yes! But of course –

FORBES: Have you seen this man before, doctor?

STEINER: Why, no – not that I am aware of.

FORBES: What about you, Bryant?

BRYANT: No, I haven't seen him before.

FORBES: You've seen Iris Archer before, naturally?

BRYANT: I was once a drama critic for one night. And I'm afraid Miss Archer was one of my – er – victims. I should like to take this opportunity of apologising.

IRIS: Save your breath!

STEINER: Mr Richmond, you must forgive me, but I am afraid I do not understand –

FORBES: My name is not Richmond, sir. It's Forbes – Sir Graham Forbes of Scotland Yard.

STEINER: Sir Graham Forbes? Scotland Yard? That explains a great deal.

BEN: It doesn't explain what the 'ell I'm doing here.

TEMPLE: I think you have a pretty good idea about that.

IRIS: Look here, Paul, this is getting beyond a joke –

TEMPLE: I'm inclined to agree, Iris – it is beyond a joke. A man was killed yesterday near Skellyfore.

IRIS: I don't know what on earth you're talking about.

The door opens and MRS WESTON enters.

MRS WESTON: This telegram has just been delivered. I'm wondering if it's meant for one of you.

FORBES: I'll take it, Mrs Weston. Thank you.

MRS WESTON: It's addressed to someone called Forbes. I said to the delivery man that no one of that name was staying here, but he insisted on leaving it.

FORBES: That's all right, Mrs Weston. Don't you worry about it. Now off you go …

SIR GRAHAM virtually pushes MRS WESTON out of the door and closes it. He hurriedly opens the telegram.

There is a pause whilst he reads it.

TEMPLE: What does it say, Sir Graham?

BEN: (*Uncomfortably*) Why the hell are you looking at me like that?

FORBES: Your name is Collins. Roy Benjamin Collins. You are wanted for the murder of a girl named Rita Allenby.

BEN: It's a lie! A lie, I tell you! You can't pin a rap on me like that. You don't have a scrap of evidence against me!

FORBES: We don't have to pin anything on you, Ben. The facts are all here.

A pause whilst BEN considers his position.

BEN: What is it you want to know?

FORBES: Where have they taken Hardwick?

BEN: I don't know. For God's sake, leave me alone!

TEMPLE: Ben, if you pull yourself together, I might be inclined to overlook this afternoon's little incident.

FORBES: Don't you see, Collins, you've got to tell us the truth sooner or later?

BEN: But I've told you. I don't know anything.

FORBES: How did you know that Temple was leaving for Aberdeen in the morning?

Another pause.

BEN: All right! All right! I'll tell you! Mrs Moffat told us. She came to the house –

FORBES: (*Surprised*) Mrs Moffat!

IRIS: (*Suddenly; desperately*) Shut up, Ben! Shut up! Keep your mouth shut, you damn fool, or …

TEMPLE: (*Quietly*) Go on, Ben …Mrs Moffat came to the house and –

BEN: She came to the house and told us that she'd received instructions from –

IRIS: Ben, for God's sake keep your mouth shut!

TEMPLE: That she had received instructions from Z.4?

BEN: Yes … from Z.4.

TEMPLE: How did Mrs Moffat receive the instructions?

BEN: I – I don't remember.

TEMPLE: (*Gently persuading*) Come on, Ben …

BEN: I don't remember I tell you! Let me get out of here!

FORBES: We've got to know how Mrs Moffat received those instructions.

BEN: (*Hysterically*) I don't know! I don't know!

STEINER: (*Interrupting*) Sir Graham …

FORBES: (*Impatiently; Angry about the interruption*) What?

STEINER: Perhaps a drink would enable him to –

BEN: Yes … get me a drink. Please get me a drink.

FORBES: Oh, very well. I'll ring the bell.

BRYANT: I can easily slip downstairs if it would help.

TEMPLE: There's no need for that, Rex. I've got my hip flask here.

TEMPLE takes his hip flask out of his jacket pocket and undoes the top.

BEN: What is it? Whisky?

TEMPLE: Yes.

BEN: You're a good man, Mr Temple.

TEMPLE: Here. Drink it.

FORBES: (*Chuckling*) I didn't know you always carry a hip flask around with you, Temple.

TEMPLE: You never know –

TEMPLE is interrupted by BEN being taken ill.

TEMPLE: Ben, what is it? What's the matter?

BEN: My throat … it's … it's …

Suddenly with a cry BEN and the flask fall to the floor.

IRIS: Oh, my God! Look at him! He's dead!

A pause.

FORBES: Yes, he's dead all right.

TEMPLE: Then I think perhaps under the circumstances you had better take care of this, Sir Graham.

TEMPLE hands SIR GRAHAM the flask.

IRIS: My God, Temple! You killed him – you killed him!

TEMPLE: (*Calmly*) I didn't kill him, Iris. Ben was killed by Z.4.

IRIS: Z.4!

FADE IN closing music.

END OF EPISODE FOUR

EPISODE FIVE

IN WHICH
MRS MOFFAT
RECEIVES A VISITOR

OPEN TO:

BEN: What is it? Whisky?
TEMPLE: Yes.
BEN: You're a good man, Mr Temple.
TEMPLE: Here. Drink it.
FORBES: (*Chuckling*) I didn't know you always carry a hip flask around with you, Temple.
TEMPLE: You never know –
TEMPLE is interrupted by BEN being taken ill.
TEMPLE: Ben, what is it? What's the matter?
BEN: My throat … it's … it's …
Suddenly with a cry BEN and the flask fall to the floor.
IRIS: Oh, my God! Look at him! He's dead!
A pause.
FORBES: Yes, he's dead all right.
TEMPLE: Then I think perhaps under the circumstances you had better take care of this, Sir Graham.
TEMPLE hands SIR GRAHAM the flask.
IRIS: My God, Temple! You killed him – you killed him!
TEMPLE: (*Calmly*) I didn't kill him, Iris. Ben was killed by Z.4.
IRIS: Z.4!
STEINER: Z.4? But I do not understand. Who is this Z.4, and what –
BRYANT: (*Interrupting STEINER*) What's in that hip flask, Sir Graham?
FORBES sniffs the hip flask.
A pause.
FORBES: Cyanide.
BRYANT: Cyanide! No wonder the poor devil went through hell.
STEINER: But surely you must have known, Mr Temple.

IRIS: Of course he knew!

TEMPLE: Doctor, do you really think I'd have given him
            that flask if I'd had any idea of the contents?

STEINER: No – no – of course not. Naturally, I would not
            dream of suggesting –

TEMPLE: (*Cutting in*) That's all right, doctor.

IRIS: It seems quite obvious to me. If Z.4 killed Ben
            – then Paul Temple is Z.4.

There is a light chuckle from SIR GRAHAM.

TEMPLE: That's certainly an interesting theory, Iris. An
            interesting theory, if nothing else.

FORBES: I agree, Temple. Maybe it wouldn't stand up to
            close examination – still, it's a theory.

IRIS: There's no need to be so damned smug about it.
            We know that Temple gave Ben the flask, and
            we know from what Mrs Moffat said that Z.4 is
            here at the inn –

IRIS stops quickly realising she has said too much.

TEMPLE: What did Mrs Moffat say?

A pause.

TEMPLE: Iris, you were about to tell us what Mrs Moffat
            said.

IRIS: Nothing. Nothing at all.

TEMPLE: Then perhaps you wouldn't mind explaining
            that remark of yours.

IRIS: If there's any explaining to be done, don't you
            think you ought to explain away this murder?
            Where did you get that flask from?

FORBES: Yes, Temple, where did you get that flask?

TEMPLE: Well, it's a long story. An uncle of mine who
            keeps an antique shop in Bangkok has a
            passion for these flasks … Chinese flasks,
            Japanese flasks, Russian flasks. It's positively
            astounding …

116

TEMPLE takes a pause and lights a cigarette.

TEMPLE: Though I suppose it isn't astounding really, because, you see, he's isn't really my uncle … after all.

IRIS: Oh really!

BRYANT laughs realising that TEMPLE has been playing for time.

FORBES: Well … er … I think we'll leave the question of the flask for the time being.

IRIS: (*Annoyed*) Why should we leave it?

TEMPLE: Just because there's a more important question, Iris.

IRIS: A more important question?

TEMPLE: Where have they taken John Hardwick?

IRIS: I don't know what you are talking about.

TEMPLE: Don't you, Iris? Don't you know? Perhaps Mrs Moffat would enlighten you.

STEINER: Mrs Moffat? Who is this Mrs Moffat?

BRYANT: I say! You don't mean the old girl in the village with the elastic-sided boots? The old dear in the sweet shop-cum-post-office?

TEMPLE: That's exactly who I mean, Rex.

BRYANT: Well, how on earth does she fit into all this?

FORBES: You know Mrs Moffat?

BRYANT: Well, I don't exactly know her. I've been in the shop once or twice, that's all.

FORBES: I see. (*A pause*) I should consider it a favour, Bryant, if you and Dr Steiner would leave us for a short while.

STEINER: Yes, yes! We are in the way, young man. Come along!

BRYANT: There's nothing like a subtle hint, is there, Temple? I presume this is one of the many occasions when the police consider it is not

117

advisable for the Press to be represented. Come along, doctor, you can buy me a large glass of your favourite lager.

BRYANT and STEINER leave and the door closes.

TEMPLE: Now, Iris –

IRIS: What's this a cue for?

TEMPLE: We want to know where they have taken John Hardwick.

IRIS: And who, precisely, are "they"?

TEMPLE: Listen, Iris, there's been quite enough beating about the bush …

IRIS: All right, let's stop beating about it.

A pause.

FORBES: Miss Archer, I don't know whether you realise it or not, but I have a warrant for your arrest.

IRIS: On what charge?

FORBES: Attempted murder.

IRIS: (*Pretending to be shocked*) What?!!

TEMPLE: The cigarette, Iris. Remember the cigarette?

IRIS: (*Angrily*) You'll never get away with that, Temple. Why, how can you prove that –

TEMPLE: (*Interrupting IRIS; calmly*) You seem to have overlooked the fact that I have a witness. Dr Steiner came into the room and caught you.

IRIS: And who the hell is Dr Steiner? It's only a case of his word against mine.

TEMPLE: It needn't be a case of anything, Iris, if you use your head.

A pause.

IRIS: What do you mean?

TEMPLE: I just want you to answer a question.

IRIS: Well?

TEMPLE: Are you Z.4?

IRIS: (*In desperation*) No!

TEMPLE: Then who is?

IRIS: I don't know.

TEMPLE: Mrs Moffat?

IRIS: I don't know, I tell you!

TEMPLE: All right. A little while ago you said "We know from what Mrs Moffat said that Z.4 is here at the inn" … How do you know that Z.4 is here?

A pause.

IRIS: (*Hesitantly*) Because Mrs Moffat received a message from Z.4.

TEMPLE: Was the message received the night before Steve and I left for Aberdeen?

IRIS: Yes.

FORBES: My God, Temple! It seems Mrs Moffat is right. Only someone staying at the inn could possibly have known that you and Steve were leaving.

TEMPLE: If Mrs Moffat isn't Z.4, does she know who Z.4 really is?

IRIS: No – not yet.

TEMPLE: I see.

FORBES: But surely Guest or van Draper must have made contact.

IRIS: No one knows the identity of Z.4, Sir Graham. Not even the infallible Paul Temple.

TEMPLE: I shouldn't be too sure of that, Iris, if I were you.

There is a knock on the door.

FORBES: That sounds like Mrs Weston. We'd better keep her out of here.

TEMPLE: It's all right – she can't see Ben from the door.

FORBES: Come in!

The door opens.

TEMPLE: Ah, Mrs Weston, it is you!

MRS WESTON: Another telegram has just arrived, Mr Temple – it's for you this time. (*A pause*) It looks as if it's been opened.

MRS WESTON hands TEMPLE the telegram.
He opens and reads it.

TEMPLE: All right, thanks, Mrs Weston. There's no reply.

TEMPLE closes the door on MRS WESTON.

FORBES: Anything important?

TEMPLE: No, not really. (*A pause*) Iris, what do you mean by saying that Mrs Moffat doesn't know who Z.4 is – yet? What does that "yet" imply?

IRIS: It can imply just what the devil you like.

TEMPLE: You've got to tell us more about Mrs Moffat.

FORBES: And you've got to tell us where they've taken Hardwick.

IRIS: I don't know where they've taken Hardwick. I've told you that already.

FORBES: And Mrs Moffat?

IRIS: There's nothing to tell you about Mrs Moffat. And if you think I'm going to spend the rest of the night going through a blasted third degree, then you're very much mistaken.

FORBES: Very well, Miss Archer, if you have no wish to answer any further questions, that's quite in order.

IRIS: (*Worried*) What's going to happen now?

FORBES: You'll spend the night here. Tomorrow, Detective Inspector Fuller will take you to Glasgow.

IRIS: Under arrest?

FORBES: Of course.

TEMPLE: Iris, don't be a damn fool! You know perfectly well what they've done with Hardwick.

IRIS: Oh, for God's sake leave me alone!

TEMPLE: I'm sorry, Iris, but we've got to find out what they've done to John Hardwick!

IRIS: I don't know! How many more times do I have to tell you?

FORBES: It's no use, Temple.

A pause.

IRIS: Since I have apparently no other alternative but to spend the night here, perhaps you will be good enough to show me to my room?

FORBES: Yes – all right.

TEMPLE: Wait a moment.

IRIS: What is it?

TEMPLE: I'd like you to know the contents of this telegram, Iris.

IRIS: It can't possibly be of interest to me.

TEMPLE: That is a matter of opinion.

FORBES: What does it say, Temple?

TEMPLE: It was handed in at Nice at five-thirty this evening. Perhaps you'd like to read it for yourself.

TEMPLE hands the telegram to IRIS.

IRIS: (*Reading*) Thanks for telegram. Information you require as follows: Hotel Martinez. Nice. April fourteenth, nineteen thirty-two.

IRIS drops the telegram to the floor.

FORBES: Look out, Temple, she's going to faint!

TEMPLE: It's all right, Sir Graham, I've got her. Let me just put her in this armchair.

FORBES: She's passed out all right.

FORBES picks up the telegram.

FORBES: (*Reading*) Hotel Martinez … Nice … April
            fourteenth, nineteen thirty-two …

FADE SCENE.
FADE IN incidental music.

FADE music.
FADE IN DETECTIVE INSPECTOR FULLER.

FULLER: And how long have we got to wait here?
CLAIKE: (*Perfectly indifferent*) Ye can't tell. That's
            impossible to say.
IRIS: I hope we won't have to stay here too long.
FULLER: They told us at Inverdale that it was a through
            train. They said nothing about us having to
            change mid-journey.
CLAIKE: Och, they must have forgotten the trains have
            been altered for the autumn schedule.
FULLER: Then it's a good job you told us to get off when
            you did.
IRIS: Do you think I might have a cigarette,
            Inspector? Or would that be asking too much?
FULLER: I'm sorry, miss. That would be against my
            instructions. Look here – are you quite certain
            that we change here for Glasgow?
CLAIKE: I'm stationmaster here, you know.
FULLER: I didn't ask you that!
CLAIKE: Ye'll be here three hours at least. The next train
            is at three-fifteen.
FULLER: Three-fifteen!
CLAIKE: That's what I said.
FULLER: But, good heavens, man, we can't stay in here
            all that time!
CLAIKE: There's always the platform, of course.
FULLER: Look here, my name's Fuller – Detective
            Inspector Fuller.

122

CLAIKE: How d'ye do? Andy Claike's the name –
            stationmaster.

IRIS: Your sparkling personality doesn't seem to
            have registered, Inspector.

FULLER: Mr Claike, I don't think you quite appreciate
            the urgency of my business.

CLAIKE: The next train to Glasgow will be at three-
            fifteen. It would still be at three-fifteen, Mr
            Fuller, if you were the Czar of Russia.

IRIS: But there isn't a Czar of Russia any longer, Mr
            Claike. Hasn't the news reached here yet?

CLAIKE: Who is this young woman? I've seen her before
            somewhere –

FULLER: Do you have a telephone here?

CLAIKE: There's one in the office. It'll cost ye –

FULLER: That's all right. Where's the office?

CLAIKE: At the end of the platform – near the slot
            machine.

FULLER: I'm going to telephone for a car. We can't stay
            here until three-fifteen – God knows when
            we'd get to Glasgow.

IRIS: You think of everything, Inspector. Anyhow,
            I'm not in any hurry.

FULLER: Well, I am! I've got a wife and kids waiting for
            me.

IRIS: It must take nerve to marry a policeman.

FULLER: Mr Claike, I want you to stay here while I
            telephone.

CLAIKE: I have my job to be getting on with, ye know.

FULLER: Is there a key to this door?

CLAIKE: Aye, there is.

FULLER: I should like it, please.

CLAIKE: But look here –

123

IRIS: It's quite all right, Mr Claike. You see, I'm a desperate criminal, so naturally the Inspector must take all the necessary precautions.

CLAIKE: Yes, well, I'm quite capable of lookin' after a wee lass – though I may not be a policeman.

A pause.

FULLER: H'm … all right. I shan't be long.

FULLER leaves and the door is closed.

IRIS: Now at least I can have that cigarette! Would you care to light it for me?

CLAIKE: Of course, Iris.

IRIS starts laughing as CLAIKE pulls off his disguise and reveals himself to really be MAJOR GUEST.

IRIS: My God! What a disguise! Darling, I could have screamed! Where's Laurence?

GUEST: He's in the office – waiting for the Inspector.

IRIS: Poor old Fuller – he's not a bad sort, if he didn't take his work so seriously. I'm afraid he's in for a warm reception. (*A pause*) Tell me, how did this all happen?

GUEST: Mrs Moffat must take the credit for the idea.

IRIS: Mrs Moffat?

GUEST: Yes. She knew the train stopped at High Moorford. Apparently this particular train always does.

IRIS: But where is the real stationmaster?

GUEST: It didn't take us long to handle poor old Claike, although young Merson was certainly a handful.

IRIS: Who's Merson?

GUEST:	He's the porter. And how that boy can wallop.
IRIS:	But what have you done with them?
GUEST:	Claike's all right. We dumped him in a goods wagon on the other side of the line. Merson, I regret to say, overstepped the bounds of discretion, so we had to put him to sleep rather forcibly.
IRIS:	Sh! There's someone coming!
GUEST:	That'll be Van.

The door opens and VAN DRAPER enters.

VAN DRAPER:	She's all right then?
IRIS:	Yes, I'm all right.
VAN DRAPER:	We'd better get away from here, Guest, and damned quickly too.
GUEST:	What's happened?
VAN DRAPER:	It's Fuller. My God, that man was a handful. The car's outside, Iris. Make straight for the chalet – you know the way. Straight through the village and bear left about a mile from Aberford.
IRIS:	But what about you and Laurence?
GUEST:	We have to see Mrs Moffat. We'll join you at the chalet later.
IRIS:	I see. Laurence …
VAN DRAPER:	Yes?
IRIS:	How did Mrs Moffat know that I should be on that particular train?
VAN DRAPER:	She received the information from Z.4.
IRIS:	Z.4 hasn't contacted her yet … personally, I mean?
VAN DRAPER:	No.

A pause.

IRIS:	Then I'll see you both later … at the chalet?
VAN DRAPER:	We shall be there about four.
IRIS:	Where's the car parked?
VAN DRAPER:	I'll take you to it.
IRIS:	Thanks. (*To GUEST*) See you later.
GUEST:	Goodbye, Iris.

VAN DRAPER and IRIS leave and the door is closed.

A pause.

GUEST paces up and down for a few moments, whistling a tune.

Suddenly the door is thrown open.

GUEST is stunned.

FULLER:	Throw that revolver on the floor! Drop it!

GUEST drops his revolver onto the floor.

GUEST:	How … how the devil did you get out?
FULLER:	Where's that other man?
GUEST:	I don't know who you're talking about.
FULLER:	Where is he? Where is the swine?
GUEST:	I tell you I don't know.
FULLER:	By God, if there's any more funny business in this place –

The door opens suddenly.

GUEST:	Look out!

A gun shot rings out.

FULLER:	Ah!

FULLER drops to the floor having been shot. He is dead.

VAN DRAPER:	It's a good job you shouted. I don't think I would have got him otherwise.
GUEST:	No – perhaps not. That shot must have echoed –
VAN DRAPER:	I doubt if it was heard above all that shunting that's going on.

GUEST:	All the same, we'd better get out of here, Van.
VAN DRAPER:	Yes, I agree.

FADE SCENE.

FADE IN the sound of a car travelling at a moderate speed.

GUEST:	Did Iris get –
VAN DRAPER:	Yes, she got away all right. The car appeared quite normal.
GUEST:	How far do you think she'll get before anything happens?
VAN DRAPER:	H'm, it's difficult to tell. Perhaps a couple of miles. The roads round here are pretty bad, you know, and she drives like the devil. She'll certainly be stepping on it at the moment – good and hard. There isn't much fear of us overtaking her just yet.
GUEST:	Van, why do you think Mrs Moffat heard from Z.4 about Iris?
VAN DRAPER:	It's perfectly obvious. Iris must have been on the verge of talking – that's why Z.4 worked out this pretty little plan.
GUEST:	And I had instructions to "doctor" the car?
VAN DRAPER:	I feel rather sorry about Iris. She had great charm if nothing else.
GUEST:	Yes. Great charm …

A pause.

GUEST:	Just a minute! That car looks familiar! Don't pass it, Van!
VAN DRAPER:	Why not?
GUEST:	It's Temple – and his wife!
VAN DRAPER:	So it is.
GUEST:	Don't pass them. We don't want to run up against Temple just now.

The car slows down.
FADE SCENE.
FADE IN incidental music.

FADE music.
FADE in the sound of a car approaching.
TEMPLE: Got any cigarettes, Steve?
STEVE: No, I'm sorry, darling, I'm completely out.
The car stops.
TEMPLE: I'll just go and buy some.
TEMPLE gets out of the car.
TEMPLE: I won't be a second.
TEMPLE then gets back into the car.
TEMPLE: I'll just move forward a bit. It's not a very safe place to park at the foot of this hill.
TEMPLE releases the handbrake.
STEVE: What time did you arrange to meet Sir Graham?
TEMPLE: I said about two. We're rather early, as a matter of fact.
STEVE: What on earth made you suggest meeting at the café at High Moorford? Surely it would have been much easier to have waited at the inn?
TEMPLE: (*Quietly*) No. I wanted to have a talk with Forbes away from the inn. I've got a funny sort of feeling about The Royal Gate …
STEVE: What do you mean?
TEMPLE: Everything that happens at the inn – every conversation that takes place there, seems by some means or other to be known to Z.4.
STEVE: Yes, that's true. They knew, for instance, that we were starting for Aberdeen and –

TEMPLE: (*Anxiously*) Look at that car coming down the hill! By Timothy, it's lurching all over the place.

STEVE: There must be something wrong with it, Paul. The steering, or –

TEMPLE: Good God! Look – it's Iris!

We hear the car travelling very fast coming towards the TEMPLES.

TEMPLE: She'll never get that car straight – she'll never do it, Steve!

STEVE: But it can't be Iris. She couldn't have got away from the detective and –

TEMPLE: There's something wrong with the steering! My God – she's going for the pavement!

A terrible collision is heard as the car mounts the pavement and crashes into a shop window at great speed. Glass is heard smashing and the horrified voices of people nearby.

STEVE: Oh my God! (*A pause*) Paul, where are you going?

TEMPLE: Wait here a second, Steve.

TEMPLE gets out of the car again and slams the door.

He crosses to where the bystanders have gathered.

TEMPLE: Excuse me, may I pass by, please? May I pass in front of you? Thank you. (*A pause*) Iris! Iris! (*A pause*) Are you all right, Iris?

IRIS: Paul, what are you doing here? (*She groans in pain*)

TEMPLE: Take it steady, Iris.

IRIS: It's nothing … Don't worry about me … It's only my shoulder … a bit of a sprain, I think … Oh …

TEMPLE: By Timothy, you're lucky to be alive!

IRIS:	There was something wrong with the steering. I could feel it as soon as – The swine! The damned swine!
TEMPLE:	How did you get off the train?
IRIS:	It stopped at High Moorford. Van Draper and Guest were waiting for me there. (*A pause*) Hell! This shoulder's worse than I thought.
TEMPLE:	Don't move, Iris. Help will be here soon.
IRIS:	All right.
TEMPLE:	Iris, they got you off that train for a very definite purpose.
IRIS:	Yes! Yes! I know! But, by God, I'll talk now all right!

The sound of an ambulance approaching can be heard in the background.

TEMPLE:	Listen, Iris, I'm going to take a chance. Get that shoulder attended to, then meet me at the Shepley Hotel, High Moorford.
IRIS:	The Shepley? All right. What time?
TEMPLE:	Let's see. I'm seeing Sir Graham at two … better make it five o'clock.
IRIS:	Five o'clock. Yes. O.K.
TEMPLE:	Take care, Iris.
IRIS:	Don't worry. I'll be there.
TEMPLE:	I hope so. I sincerely hope so.

FADE SCENE.

FADE IN STEVE's voice.

STEVE:	Was she badly hurt?
TEMPLE:	No, it doesn't look like it's very serious. She had a very lucky escape.

TEMPLE gets into the car.

TEMPLE:	By Jove, we'll have to move, or we'll be late.
STEVE:	What about the cigarettes?

TEMPLE: There's no time now – we'll get them in High Moorford.

STEVE: What was the matter with Iris's car?

TEMPLE: She seemed to think it had been "fixed".

STEVE: But, Paul, who would do that?

TEMPLE: Ah, perhaps she'll enlighten us when we see her later on.

STEVE: Later on?

TEMPLE: Yes, we're meeting at the Shepley Hotel.

STEVE: Do you think she'll be well enough to make it?

TEMPLE: I have every reason to believe so.

TEMPLE starts the car and it drives off.
FADE SCENE.

FADE IN SIR GRAHAM's voice.

FORBES: It's no good. We've had no luck. I'm damned if we can find that chalet. We've got to find out from Iris, Temple. Without her help we'll never be able to find the place.

STEVE: Didn't you say that you were going to put Inspector Sandford on the case?

FORBES: Sandford's been on the lake since ten this morning. He knows this district like the palm of his hand, but I'm damned if he can spot their hideout.

TEMPLE: I suppose you've got someone up at Skerry Lodge?

FORBES: Good lord, yes! The house is practically surrounded – though I'm afraid it's a case of shutting the stable door after the horse has bolted. I've got a man watching Mrs Moffat's shop too, though I've given him strict instructions to keep well in the background. I thought it might be quite a good idea to allow

131

the old girl plenty of rope – if she really is mixed up with this gang – then there's just a possibility that she might lead us to the chalet.

TEMPLE: There's an old saying that if you give a Scotsman enough rope he'll start making cigars! And you can rely on Mrs Moffat to be pretty canny. She's mixed up in this all right, and I have a hunch that when Z.4 does contact the gang, it will be through Mrs Moffat.

FORBES: But how the devil will she recognise Z.4 if they have never met?

TEMPLE: Quite simply, Sir Graham. Z.4 has obviously supplied Mrs Moffat with some sort of password.

FORBES: I know. But somehow I can't bring myself to believe that the gang are still ignorant of Z.4's identity. Surely by now van Draper must know it – or possibly Guest.

TEMPLE: No, I don't believe any of them know who Z.4 really is.

FORBES: Well, if that's the case, how the devil can Z.4 be absolutely certain that he isn't going to be double-crossed?

STEVE: They can't very well double-cross Z.4 if they don't know who Z.4 really is.

FORBES: I don't mean it in that sense, Steve. What I mean is, that they could refuse to take the slightest notice of Z.4's instructions if –

TEMPLE: And so they would, if it wasn't for that one little factor you seem to be overlooking –

FORBES: What's that?

TEMPLE: Blackmail!

STEVE: You said yourself, Sir Graham, that Z.4 knew something about each member of the organisation.

FORBES: That's only a theory, Steve. And I'm beginning to doubt if it was a very sound one.

TEMPLE: On the contrary, Sir Graham, the theory was excellent.

FORBES: What makes you so certain?

TEMPLE: Merely the fact that I happened to discover the little something that Iris was hoping to conceal and that she felt sure only Z.4 knew about.

FORBES: What?!

TEMPLE: Do you remember the telegram I received?

FORBES: "Hotel Martinez ... Nice ... April fourteenth, nineteen thirty-two." Yes, what about it?

TEMPLE: Well, that telegram proved to Iris beyond a shadow of doubt that Z.4 was not the only person who knew her secret.

FORBES: All the same, she didn't talk – in spite of the telegram.

TEMPLE: No, she didn't talk – then. But I think she will.

FORBES: Well, we shall hear all about that when we get Iris to Glasgow.

STEVE: Paul, you're being very mysterious about your previous telegram. What exactly did it mean?

FORBES: Yes, I've been wondering about that, Temple.

TEMPLE: Sir Graham, when you told me that, in your opinion, Z.4 had some sort of hold over each member of the organisation, I made up my mind to discover just what it was that Iris was anxious to conceal.

FORBES: And did you?

TEMPLE: In nineteen thirty-two Iris married a young stockbroker by the name of Forrester. They

133

spent their honeymoon – or part of it – at the Martinez Hotel in Nice. On April the fourteenth, two days after they had arrived at the hotel, Forrester was found dead. To all intents and purposes it was suicide. But –

FORBES: But – what?

TEMPLE: Yes, Sir Graham, there was a "but", and a rather unpleasant one, I'm afraid, so far as Iris was concerned.

FORBES: But, damn it all, Temple, surely we'd have heard about this. Iris Archer isn't exactly a nonentity.

TEMPLE: Not at the present time. But in nineteen thirty-two Iris was known by the somewhat more fanciful name of Rosie Shiner.

FORBES: Rosie Shiner?

STEVE: But what happened about Forrester?

TEMPLE takes some press clippings out of his wallet.

TEMPLE: The whole business as far as I can gather from the French authorities – and also from these press clippings – is a bit of a mix-up. Iris wasn't actually accused of the murder, but the authorities had a nasty sort of suspicion that she was mixed up in it. The most important witness, however – an English chambermaid who happened to be working at the hotel – suddenly disappeared, and after a short while the matter was more or less dropped.

FORBES: M'm … Well, all this certainly seems to do away with the suspicion that Iris might be Z.4.

TEMPLE: Iris isn't Z.4, Sir Graham. I'm certain on that point.

FORBES: Then who the devil is? D'you reckon it's Steiner?

134

TEMPLE: But we know who Steiner is, don't we, Sir Graham? He's a Professor of Philosophy at the University of Philadelphia.

FORBES: M'm … that's what he would have us believe. (*A pause*) Of course, there's Rex Bryant. I'm damned if I can make Bryant out, Temple.

STEVE: Yes, after all, we did find his watch chain on Ernie Weston.

TEMPLE: That isn't necessarily an indication that Bryant was implicated – in Weston's murder, I mean.

FORBES: Good heavens, Temple, he must be mixed up in this business somehow or other! Otherwise how the devil did Weston get hold of the watch chain in the first place?

TEMPLE: I don't think there's any doubt about that. He helped himself to it. Just as he helped himself to Steiner's cufflinks and Lady Retford's ring.

FORBES: Lady Retford's ring?

STEVE: How do you know the ring belonged to Lady Retford, darling?

TEMPLE: I made enquiries at the local police station. Quite an obvious procedure, eh, Sir Graham? They told me that Lady Retford stayed at The Royal Gate about a fortnight ago. She was only there for a week, but Ernie managed to get hold of the ring all right. Poor old Ernie was an opportunist, if nothing else.

FORBES: Yes, but what the devil does all this prove? Merely that Ernie Weston was a sort of common pickpocket.

STEVE: It certainly doesn't explain the identity of Z.4.

FORBES: And another thing, Temple, if Weston was just an ordinary little kleptomaniac and didn't have a row with Rex Bryant, and wasn't mixed up with all this other business – who the devil killed him?

TEMPLE: (*Calmly*) Z.4.

FORBES: But why? In heaven's name … why?

TEMPLE: Your guess is as good as mine, Sir Graham.

FORBES: But what is your guess, Temple?

TEMPLE: My guess is this. The moment I arrived at the inn, Weston went through my pockets and found the letter that Lindsay – or Hammond if you like – had given me. Later, realising that the letter might be of some personal value to me, he returned it. You may remember that the letter was pushed under the door.

FORBES: Yes, but that doesn't explain why he was murdered.

TEMPLE: Doesn't it? Well, this is my theory, Sir Graham. After he had returned the letter, the poor devil must have mentioned the fact to someone, and unfortunately for him that someone happened to be Z.4. Naturally, Z.4 wanted the letter before it got into your hands. It was, in fact, absolutely imperative that Hammond's message shouldn't reach you. And yet Ernie Weston, after having had possession of the letter, had calmly returned it. By Timothy, you can imagine how Z.4 felt about it!

FORBES: My God, yes! It's certainly a motive.

STEVE: But Weston couldn't have known anything at all about Z.4, or he'd have understood the message.

TEMPLE: Exactly.

FORBES: Look here, Temple! Supposing Bryant started questioning Weston about the watch chain. Weston got a bit nervous, begins to suspect

Bryant was some sort of police officer, and without thinking started telling him about the letter. Bryant would naturally put two and two together and –

STEVE: (*Interrupting TEMPLE*) The same thing applies to Dr Steiner, Sir Graham. He may have questioned Weston about his cufflinks. Weston may have broken down, as you suggest, and then, without realising its significance, mentioned the letter. Incidentally, Steiner could have been responsible for Bryant's watch chain disappearing, planting it on Weston in order to throw suspicion on to Bryant.

TEMPLE: By Timothy, we'll make a detective of you yet, Steve.

STEVE: Thank you, darling.

FORBES: Seriously, Temple, don't you think Steiner is Z.4?

TEMPLE: (*Avoiding the question*) I think it's about time we got back to The Royal Gate, Sir Graham. Perhaps Sandford has some news by now.

FORBES: (*Realising that TEMPLE won't say anything*) Yes, that might be for the best. No, no, never mind, Temple, I'll pay.

WAITRESS: Three shillings, please.

FORBES: Here we are. Keep the change.

WAITRESS: Thank you.

TEMPLE, STEVE and FORBES leave the café and start to walk along the street.

FORBES: By the way, I see the Golden Clipper had a pretty rough trip the other day. What was it like when you came across?

STEVE: It was perfect, Sir Graham. We enjoyed every minute of it, didn't we, Paul?

137

TEMPLE: Every minute.

FORBES: I wish to God I could get away for a month or so. I've never been to the States.

STEVE: You'd love it.

FORBES: Oh well, we might think of it in about a couple of years. I've always wanted to travel. As our friend Mrs Moffat would say, "What was it Shakespeare said about travellers?" Is that your car over there, Temple?

TEMPLE doesn't reply.

STEVE: What is it, darling?

TEMPLE: Did Mrs Moffat use those actual words, Sir Graham – "What was it Shakespeare said about travellers?"

FORBES: (*A little uncertain*) Why, yes … yes, I think so.

TEMPLE: When? When did she say it?

FORBES: Why, the first time I went into the shop. But I can't for the life of me see what you're driving at.

TEMPLE: By Timothy, what a fool! What an utter fool I've been!

STEVE: Darling, what is it?

TEMPLE: Don't you see, Steve? Mrs Moffat said exactly the same thing to me. "What was it Shakespeare said about travellers?" If I had given the right answer – or if you'd have given it, Sir Graham – she'd have thought we were Z.4!

FORBES: My God! You mean that's the password?

TEMPLE: (*Thinking aloud*) Travellers … what is the quotation? Do you remember it, Steve?

STEVE: No, not offhand. But look, there's a bookshop just over there. I'm sure we could look the quotation up there.

FADE SCENE.
FADE IN incidental music.

FADE music.
FADE IN MRS MOFFAT's voice.

MRS MOFFAT: Ye mustn't stay long. There's a man watching the place.

GUEST: What?!!

MRS MOFFAT: It's all right. The nearest telephone is half a mile away from here, so it'd be quite a while before he could get a message through. (*A pause*) What happened about Iris?

GUEST: It came off all right. We've just passed her car halfway through a shop window. Must have been a hell of a smash … they told us she'd been taken to hospital nearly dead.

MRS MOFFAT: She was a bonnie lass – and useful, too. But Z.4 can take no chances.

GUEST: Have you heard from Z.4?

MRS MOFFAT: Not yet.

VAN DRAPER: The screen is completed. Hardwick's finished now. Why the devil doesn't Z.4 come out into the open?

MRS MOFFAT: Don't worry – he will. Ye just have to be patient.

GUEST: He? (*Quietly*) Has it occurred to you that Z.4 might be a woman?

MRS MOFFAT: Maybe.

GUEST: Well, the sooner this business is all wound up, the better I'll like it. The police have been searching thro' the damned chalet all day long. It's getting too warm to be pleasant.

MRS MOFFAT: Don't worry, they won't find the chalet very easily.

GUEST: I know that. But Hardwick is getting disagreeable again.

VAN DRAPER: One thing is for certain, when Z.4 comes out into the open, the financial side of the business must be pretty well cleared up. He isn't making a move until he's obviously certain there's a market for the screen – that's obvious.

MRS MOFFAT: There's no lack of markets. Practically every country in Europe has been bitten by the rearmament bug.

A pause.

VAN DRAPER: You seem pretty well informed, Mrs Moffat.

MRS MOFFAT: Of course I'm well informed. I use my own common sense.

VAN DRAPER: I see. (*A pause*) Well, come along, Guest, we'd better get back to the chalet.

GUEST: Yes, all right.

VAN DRAPER: The moment Z.4 arrives –

MRS MOFFAT: (*Interrupting VAN DRAPER*) The moment Z.4 arrives, we shall both come down to the chalet.

GUEST: Yes, yes … well then …

The shop door opens, the shop bell is heard and the door closes again after VAN DRAPER and GUEST have left.
A car is heard driving off.

MRS MOFFAT: Ach, I don't know …

The shop door opens and the bell is heard again. REX BRYANT enters and closes the door behind him.

MRS MOFFAT: Hello, sir.

BRYANT: (*Cheerfully*) Good afternoon.

MRS MOFFAT: Good afternoon, sir, what can I get you?

BRYANT looks round the shop for a moment.

BRYANT: I'd like some razor blades, please. Do you have any of the Pride of the Regiment brand?

MRS MOFFAT: No, I'm afraid I haven't.

BRYANT: Good lord, you should always keep a stock of Pride of the Regiment blades. I wouldn't shave with anything else. Makes your face as smooth as a baby's – I say, old girl, you'll know me the next time you see me and no mistake.

MRS MOFFAT: You've been here before haven't ye?

BRYANT: Yes, once or twice. I always patronise the small trader if I can.

MRS MOFFAT: Where do ye come from now?

BRYANT: Where do I come from now? I come from Chelsea, Mrs Moffat. Gay old Chelsea. Where girls are girls and men are … well, that's a moot point.

MRS MOFFAT: Chelsea? That'd be a long way, I'm thinkin'.

BRYANT: You think quite rightly. It's fairly near a place called London.

MRS MOFFAT: I've a married sister in London. Peckham, I think it is. Is there a place called Peckham?

BRYANT: Yes, there is a place called Peckham.

MRS MOFFAT: Aye, I thought there was. (*A pause*) It must be a wonderful thing to travel. Often wish I had the time. And the money, of course. What was it Shakespeare said about travellers?

BRYANT: I think the exact words were: "Travellers ne'er did lie, though fools at home condemn 'em". (*A pause*) "Travellers ... ne'er ... did lie ..." Mrs Moffat!

MRS MOFFAT: (*In awe and reverence*) Z.4!

FADE IN closing music.

END OF EPISODE FIVE

EPISODE SIX

INTRODUCING
Z.4

OPEN TO: *The sound of the shop door opening and the bell ringing. REX BRYANT enters and closes the door behind him.*

MRS MOFFAT: Hello, sir.

BRYANT: (*Cheerfully*) Good afternoon.

MRS MOFFAT: Good afternoon, sir, what can I get you?

BRYANT looks round the shop for a moment.

BRYANT: I'd like some razor blades, please. Do you have any of the Pride of the Regiment brand?

MRS MOFFAT: No, I'm afraid I haven't.

BRYANT: Good lord, you should always keep a stock of Pride of the Regiment blades. I wouldn't shave with anything else. Makes your face as smooth as a baby's – I say, old girl, you'll know me the next time you see me and no mistake.

MRS MOFFAT: You've been here before haven't ye?

BRYANT: Yes, once or twice. I always patronise the small trader if I can.

MRS MOFFAT: Where do ye come from now?

BRYANT: Where do I come from now? I come from Chelsea, Mrs Moffat. Gay old Chelsea. Where girls are girls and men are … well, that's a moot point.

MRS MOFFAT: Chelsea? That'd be a long way, I'm thinkin'.

BRYANT: You think quite rightly. It's fairly near a place called London.

MRS MOFFAT: I've a married sister in London. Peckham, I think it is. Is there a place called Peckham?

BRYANT: Yes, there is a place called Peckham.

145

MRS MOFFAT: Aye, I thought there was. (*A pause*) It must be a wonderful thing to travel. Often wish I had the time. And the money, of course. What was it Shakespeare said about travellers?

BRYANT: I think the exact words were: "Travellers ne'er did lie, though fools at home condemn 'em". (*A pause*) "Travellers … ne'er … did lie …" Mrs Moffat!

MRS MOFFAT: (*In awe and reverence*) Z.4!

BRYANT: (*Softly*) Yes … Z.4.

MRS MOFFAT: (*Very excited*) Oh, we've been waiting for ye! My God, how we've waited! I was beginning to think ye'd leave it too late.

BRYANT: (*Calmly*) Can't we go into the back parlour? It's rather difficult talking here. Too dangerous.

MRS MOFFAT: Why, yes, of course! Just a moment and I'll just bolt the door.

MRS MOFFAT crosses and bolts the shop door.

MRS MOFFAT: You never know, someone might have tried to come in. Prudence is everything I always say. Walls have ears and all that. Come along, this way. Mind the first step, it's a bit tricky.

They go into the back room.

MRS MOFFAT: We followed out your instructions about Iris.

BRYANT: About Iris?

MRS MOFFAT: Why, of course – about Iris and the car.

BRYANT: Oh yes, about Iris and the car … now let's see –

MRS MOFFAT: But surely you remember.

146

BRYANT:	Yes, yes, of course. I was thinking of something else. (*A pause*) How is Iris?
MRS MOFFAT:	We haven't heard. Not yet.
BRYANT:	Oh, I see. And Hardwick?
MRS MOFFAT:	The screen is finished.
BRYANT:	Good.
MRS MOFFAT:	How are things at your end? Are the arrangements complete?
BRYANT:	Yes. Quite complete. Did you have much trouble with Hardwick?
MRS MOFFAT:	Not at first. He was too bitter about things. Now he seems rather difficult.
BRYANT:	Difficult?
MRS MOFFAT:	Yes. At times he gets almost violent. The poor devil can't understand why we moved him to the chalet.
BRYANT:	No. I suppose he can't. (*A pause*) How far do you reckon the chalet is from here?
MRS MOFFAT:	(*Surprised*) How far? But ye know where the chalet is as well as I do!
BRYANT:	Of course, but I've never actually been there.
MRS MOFFAT:	Never been there! But ye had the place made ready for us! It was ye who – (*Horrified*) My God! You're not Z.4!
BRYANT:	(*Calmly*) I'm sorry to disappoint you, Mrs Moffat, but you are quite right. I am not Z.4.

MRS MOFFAT makes a sudden move towards the door.

BRYANT:	Stand away from that door! If I were you, Mrs Moffat, I should sit down. I'd hate to spoil this perfectly good suit by shooting through the jacket pocket.
MRS MOFFAT:	Who are you? Who the devil –

147

BRYANT: (*Curtly*) All in good time, Mrs Moffat, all
                 in good time.

BRYANT looks round the room.

BRYANT: Is that telephone switched through?

MRS MOFFAT doesn't reply.

BRYANT: Mrs Moffat, don't forget I'm pointing a
                 gun at you. Now, is this telephone
                 switched through.

MRS MOFFAT: (*Reluctantly*) Aye. Aye, it is.

BRYANT lifts the receiver.

BRYANT: (*Into the phone*) Hello … Inverdale 83,
                 please … yes, 83 … (*He waits*) Now, Mrs
                 Moffat, perhaps you'll have the goodness
                 to tell me more about the chalet.

MRS MOFFAT: I'll tell ye nothing.

BRYANT: My dear Mrs – (*His call is put through;
                 into the phone*) Hello … Inverdale 83? …
                 Is that The Royal Gate? … Will you get
                 Mr Temple at once? … Yes, Mr Paul
                 Temple. (*He waits and turns to MRS
                 MOFFAT again*) There's nothing like
                 patience, is there, Mrs Moffat? Nothing
                 like patience …

FADE SCENE.
FADE IN incidental music.

FADE music.
FADE IN SIR GRAHAM's voice.

FORBES: I'm expecting a telephone call from
                 Wright, one of my Inspectors, otherwise
                 I'd go back to my room and snatch forty
                 winks.

STEVE: Who exactly is Inspector Wright, Sir
                 Graham?

FORBES:	He's the fellow I've got watching Mrs Moffat's place.
TEMPLE:	Oh, yes. I'd almost forgotten about him.
STEVE:	(*Suddenly*) Hello, Mrs Weston. Going out?
MRS WESTON:	Aye, just down to the village.
STEVE:	It'll be a nice walk.
MRS WESTON:	It doesn't look too bright to me. There's a mist coming down the mountain.
STEVE:	Oh, I think it'll be all right. I'd take my chances if I were you.
MRS WESTON:	Well, I do hope so, I'm sure.

The door opens and ALEC enters.

MRS WESTON:	Yes, Alec, what is it?
ALEC:	Telephone.
MRS WESTON:	Who's it for?
ALEC:	Don't know.
MRS WESTON:	Didn't you ask? (*A pause*) Oh, never mind, I'll find out.

MRS WESTON and ALEC exit.

STEVE:	Looks like it's your call, Sir Graham.
FORBES:	Yes, I hope so.

A pause then MRS WESTON returns.

MRS WESTON:	It's for Mr Temple. You can take it in the hall.
TEMPLE:	Thank you.

TEMPLE leaves.

MRS WESTON:	Ah, well, I'd better be off. I think mebbe I'll take my umbrella after all, just to be on the safe side.

MRS WESTON leaves.

FORBES:	Mrs Weston seems to have taken things rather well, doesn't she?
STEVE:	Yes. She does rather …
FORBES:	It hadn't occurred to me before.

STEVE: I wonder what she really thinks about all
                    this. After all, when two men are murdered
                    under your very nose as it were – and one
                    of them happens to be your husband into
                    the bargain, then surely –

The door opens and DR STEINER enters.

STEINER: Good afternoon, Mrs Temple. Good
                    afternoon, sir.

FORBES: Good afternoon, doctor. Just out for a
                    stroll?

STEINER: Ja. Ja wenn man ein bischen dick ist muss
                    man abend spazieren gehen …

FORBES: And what does that mean, doctor?

STEINER: It means that when one is fat one should
                    take plenty of exercise.

*SIR GRAHAM grunts – clearly not impressed with the
inference.*

STEINER: We shall meet later, I hope … at dinner?

STEVE: Of course.

STEINER: Then for the time being – auf weidersehen.

STEINER leaves and closes the door.

FORBES: I'm damned if I can make head or tail of
                    that fellow.

The door opens and TEMPLE returns.

STEVE: Oh, here's Paul again.

FORBES: Well?

TEMPLE: That was Bryant.

FORBES: Where is he?

TEMPLE: He's at Mrs Moffat's.

FORBES: Rex Bryant is? What the devil is he doing
                    there?

TEMPLE: Well, I'm rather afraid I sent him there.

FORBES: (*Astonished*) You sent him there?

TEMPLE: I did indeed.

150

STEVE: But, darling, why?

TEMPLE: Immediately I realised that we knew the true significance of the quotation – in other words, the means by which Z.4 intended to contact the organisation – I telephoned Bryant.

STEVE: What was the point of that?

TEMPLE: I instructed him to visit Mrs Moffat's, and by means of the quotation pass himself off as Z.4.

STEVE: Then Rex isn't Z.4?

TEMPLE: Of course not.

FORBES: Well, what's happened?

TEMPLE: I was hoping that Mrs Moffat might be completely taken in by Rex, and divulge the exact whereabouts of the chalet. Unfortunately, that scheme hasn't worked out quite as well as I anticipated.

STEVE: Mrs Moffat hasn't escaped?

TEMPLE: Oh no. Rex is taking care of that all right. I lent him a revolver – he said he would be scared stiff to use it, but I expect he looks the part all right.

FORBES: Then there's nothing to worry about. Z.4 is still bound to contact Mrs Moffat. We'll get Z.4, Temple, if I have to arrest the whole village!

TEMPLE: I hardly think that will be necessary, Sir Graham.

FORBES: (*Suddenly*) Look here, we'd better join Bryant as soon as we possibly can. For all we know Z.4 might turn up at Mrs Moffat's while we are hanging around here.

TEMPLE: I'll leave that to you, Sir Graham. I've got an appointment at High Moorford which is rather important.

FORBES: An appointment at High Moorford?

TEMPLE: Yes.

FORBES: Who with?

TEMPLE: With Iris Archer.

FORBES: You're joking!

TEMPLE: I'm not.

FORBES: You don't mean to say Iris escaped from the train?

TEMPLE: I'm afraid so. Van Draper and Guest had a car waiting for her. The car was tampered with so that the steering collapsed about twenty minutes after she'd started.

FORBES: Good God! What happened?

TEMPLE: Fortunately, Iris escaped with just a pretty bad shaking. She's meeting me at the Shepley Hotel, Moorford. That trick with the car didn't exactly please Iris, Sir Graham.

FORBES: You think she'll talk?

TEMPLE: I'm sure of it.

FORBES: (*Excitedly*) Things are looking up, Temple! Even if we can't find out about the chalet from Mrs Moffat, we still have another string to our bow.

TEMPLE: We'll find the chalet all right. You see, van Draper and Guest visited Mrs Moffat's shop, and according to Rex, who arrived on the scene just as they were leaving, your man is tailing them. That's why he hasn't telephoned.

FORBES: So if Draper and Guest are on their way to the chalet, Wright can't miss it. Things certainly are looking up!

STEVE: Paul, it's nearly five.

TEMPLE: Yes, of course. We'll meet you at Mrs Moffatt's in about an hour, Sir Graham.

STEVE: Why at Mrs Moffatt's?

TEMPLE: Because Mrs Moffat is expecting Z.4. And I'd rather like to be there when Z.4 arrives!

FADE SCENE.
FADE IN incidental music.

FADE music.
FADE IN the sound of a car driving at great speed.

GUEST: The roads are slippery.

VAN DRAPER: Yes, you'd better take it easy. There's no need to drive so fast.

A pause.

GUEST: Is that car still behind us?

VAN DRAPER: Yes.

GUEST: (*Nervously*) He's been behind us ever since we left the shop. I don't like it.

VAN DRAPER: You just concentrate on the road. If he tries any funny business just leave him to me.

GUEST: Yes, all right.

VAN DRAPER: How much further is it?

GUEST: We're not even in Aberford yet.

A pause.

VAN DRAPER: I wonder what happened to Iris.

GUEST: She can't have survived what happened to that car.

VAN DRAPER: Can't we stop in Aberford and buy an evening paper? There might be something about it in there.

GUEST: I hope everything is all right at the chalet.

VAN DRAPER: What do you mean?

GUEST: Hardwick was in a terrible mood when we left. I got the impression he was on the point of snapping …

VAN DRAPER: Don't worry about that – he'll be ok. (*Chuckling*) If you'd seen how I tied him up, you would have ... (*He stops chuckling*)

GUEST: (*Anxiously*) What's the matter?

VAN DRAPER: That car is still behind us. I thought he would have stayed on the main road when we turned off. He's definitely following us.

GUEST: (*Anxiously*) What should we do now, do you think?

VAN DRAPER: Drive a little slower. If he comes alongside ram into him and run him off the road.

GUEST: (*Bewildered*) But Van, we can't ...

VAN DRAPER: (*Wildly*) Do as I say!

GUEST: (*Softly, after a pause*) O.K. whatever you say.

VAN DRAPER: (*Shouting*) Now! Pull over to the left! Now! Be quick!

GUEST: Watch out, we're skidding!

VAN DRAPER: Holy shit! What's happening?!!!

There is a giant smack of the cars against each other followed by a crashing of glass.

This is followed by a pause.

GUEST: (*Moving convulsively with great difficulty*) Ah ... oh ... van Draper, are you all right? (*A pause*) Van? (*Suddenly, desperately*) Van Draper! Van Draper! (*Softly*) Good grief, he's ... dead.

FADE SCENE.
FADE IN dramatic incidental music.

FADE music.
FADE IN a HOTEL CLERK speaking.

CLERK: Good afternoon, sir.

GUEST: Good afternoon. Could I have a room, please? A single room if you have one. I may be staying for a day or two.

CLERK: Very good, sir. Let me just check. (*A pause*) Ah yes, that will be room fourteen.

GUEST: Thank you. And could you let me have a large double Scotch sent up to my room straight away? Oh, and I shall want dinner in my room – about seven-thirty.

CLERK: Very good, sir.

The CLERK rings a bell.

CLERK: If you wouldn't mind signing the register, sir.

GUEST: Of course.

A pause.

CLERK: Thank you very much, Major Guest. The room is on the first floor.

GUEST: Thank you. Oh, and make that a bottle of Scotch, would you?

CLERK: Very good, sir.

FADE SCENE.

FADE IN GUEST's voice.

GUEST: Thank you. Put my suitcase over there, please.

PORTER: Yes, sir.

GUEST: Here, that's for you.

PORTER: Thank you, sir.

The PORTER leaves and the door closes.

A pause.

GUEST opens his suitcase.

Suddenly the door opens and closes again.

GUEST: (*Who thinks he's seen a ghost*) Iris! How the devil did you get here?

IRIS: Surprised, Major?

155

GUEST: What – what happened?

IRIS: Don't worry, your little trick with the steering worked all right. There was a most spectacular accident that would have cheered you immensely – drop that gun!

GUEST drops the gun he is holding. IRIS picks it up.

IRIS: Following instructions to the last.

GUEST: (*Nervously*) Iris ... things are serious, damned serious.

IRIS: What do you mean?

GUEST: After you left us at the station, Van and I went to Mrs Moffat's place; then about two hours ago we went to the chalet.

IRIS: I don't see that this interests me particularly.

GUEST: We were followed, Iris. They've had a man watching the shop for the past week.

IRIS: Go on.

GUEST: The man caught up with us about a mile from Aberford, and the two cars – My God, there was a crash! I thought at first –

IRIS: A dose of your own medicine, eh? Go on.

GUEST: Van was killed – almost instantaneously, I should imagine. The other fellow was pretty badly cut about, but his car was all right, so I continued the journey alone.

IRIS: To the chalet?

GUEST: Yes. When I got to the boat, I noticed some smoke rising round the headland, and by the time I got the boat across Skellydown loch the whole place was practically in ruins.

IRIS: How on earth could that happen?

GUEST: When Van and I received our instructions about taking you off the train at High Moorford, we left Hardwick at the chalet alone. He couldn't escape – we made certain of that all right, but we never dreamt that he'd set fire to the place.

IRIS: Then what's happened to the screen and the beam? And Hardwick too, for that matter?

GUEST: I don't think there's any doubt about what happened to Hardwick … Standing at the side of the lake staring at what was left of the chalet, I suddenly felt desperate and hellishly scared. I knew that Z.4 was on the verge of contacting Mrs Moffat. I knew that sooner or later van Draper would be found, and the net would begin to tighten. I came back over the lake, and decided to stay here for a while and wait for things to develop.

IRIS: They'll develop all right.

GUEST: In a day or two I expect I'll go back to town.

IRIS: Will you, Major? That's very interesting.

GUEST: What do you mean?

IRIS: Simply this. If it hadn't been for a miracle, I shouldn't be here. You did your damnedest to get rid of me, and I always make a point of paying my debts.

GUEST: Iris …

IRIS: You needn't try any fancy tricks.

GUEST: What are you going to do?

A pause.

IRIS: Strange though it may seem, Major, I'm going to keep you here until a friend of mine arrives.

GUEST: Friend? What friend?

IRIS: I think you'll find him excellent company. I'm referring to Temple.

GUEST: Paul Temple! Why, you dirty, double-crossing little –

GUEST makes a move towards IRIS.

157

IRIS: Stay back, Major. I'm not afraid to use this!

GUEST: But, Iris, you can't …

IRIS: Whether you like it or not, Major, you are going to wait for Paul Temple!

FADE SCENE.
FADE IN incidental music.

FADE music.
FADE IN SIR GRAHAM talking.

FORBES: I thought you were on a bit of a wild goose chase.

TEMPLE: Nothing of the kind. Guest turning up satisfied Iris's lust for revenge. She got even with him. That's what Iris wanted, Sir Graham.

FORBES: What time is it, Temple?

TEMPLE: I make it about seven-twenty.

STEVE: That's right, darling. I put my watch right by the radio in the car.

FORBES: Heavens, I've been here for over two hours!

MRS MOFFAT: And how much longer do ye intend to stay? Hanging about like a lot o' sheep. I'll hae ye know that the shop closes at eight and –

FORBES: I think you know why we are staying, Mrs Moffat. And you might as well make the best of it. We're here until Z.4 arrives.

MRS MOFFAT: Then for God's sake let's go into the shop. We can't all stay in here. If you don't get some air into this room I shall pass out on ye.

STEVE: It is pretty stuffy, Sir Graham.

158

FORBES: I know. But we can see the door from here
                 without being noticed. Besides, the shop
                 must appear to be empty, otherwise Z.4
                 will never come out into the open.

TEMPLE: We've no guarantee that he will. Recent
                 events might have changed his plans.

FORBES: Yes, there is that possibility. But somehow
                 I've a feeling that he's going to put in an
                 appearance, and pretty soon.

STEVE: What happened to Rex, Sir Graham?

FORBES: I sent him back to the inn. There was no
                 point in Rex staying here. Besides, he was
                 rather anxious to make a start on writing
                 up his story. Maybe he's gone down to the
                 chalet to see if –

The telephone starts to ring.

FORBES lifts the receiver.

FORBES: (*Into the phone*) Hello? ... Oh, it's you,
                 Murphy ... Yes? ... That's fine ... Good
                 ... Well, mind you keep your eyes
                 skinned, and don't hesitate to challenge
                 anybody. It doesn't matter a damn who
                 they are!

FORBES slams down the receiver.

FORBES: That was one of my men phoning from the
                 box down the road. This shop's guarded
                 like the Tower of London. Once we get
                 Z.4 in here he'll never –

The shop door opens and the door bell rings.

TEMPLE: (*Interrupting FORBES*) Sh!

STEVE: It's Dr Steiner!

FORBES: You know what to do, Mrs Moffat. And
                 don't forget that quotation. There must be
                 no mistake.

TEMPLE: He's waiting, Mrs Moffat.

MRS MOFFAT moves through into the shop.

MRS MOFFAT: (*Somewhat nervously*) Good evening, sir.

STEINER: Good evening. I should like some postcards, please.

MRS MOFFAT: Certainly. Would ye like plain post cards or –

STEINER: Picture postcards, please.

MRS MOFFAT: You're … you're a stranger round these parts?

STEINER: Very much so, I'm afraid. From Philadelphia, U.S.A.

MRS MOFFAT: Philadelphia! That must be an awful long way?

STEINER: Well, it rather depends where you start from. (*He laughs*) Ah, yes. I was forgetting – the postcards. How much?

MRS MOFFAT: Sixpence.

STEINER: Thank you.

A pause.

MRS MOFFAT: Philadelphia. It must be a wonderful thing to travel. I often wish I had the time – and the money, of course. What was it that Shakespeare said about travellers?

Another pause.

STEINER: (*Chuckling*) I can't recall offhand, madam. But I think we can take it for granted that it was not very much to the point. (*A pause*) Sixpence, I think you said?

MRS MOFFAT: That's right.

STEINER: Ah, your English coins are so – elusive … Yes, here we are … Sixpence.

MRS MOFFAT: Thank ye.

STEINER: Goodnight, madam.

160

MRS MOFFAT: Goodnight.

The doorbell rings again as STEINER leaves. The door closes.

FORBES: (*Bewildered*) Well, I'm damned!

MRS MOFFAT: I hope ye're satisfied.

A clock strikes eight.

MRS MOFFAT: I'll be closin' the shop now – or maybe the police will fine me for breaking the regulations.

TEMPLE: Just a minute, Mrs Moffat, I think that clock is five minutes fast.

MRS MOFFAT: (*Annoyed*) Oh!

The shop door opens again and the bell rings.

FORBES: There's someone else!

STEVE: (*Indifferently*) Oh, it's only Mrs Weston.

FORBES: Now what the devil does she want?

Conversation in shop.

MRS WESTON: Good evening, Mrs Moffat.

MRS MOFFAT: Good evening, Mrs Weston. Shocking weather we're havin'.

MRS WESTON: Aye, I can't remember a worse winter than this, and that's the truth. We seem to have had nothing but rain since August.

MRS MOFFAT: I was sorry to hear about your husband – it must have been an awful shock to ye.

MRS WESTON: (*With a sigh*) I don't suppose anyone will ever know just how much I miss him. There are moments when I catch myself … (*Suddenly with a sigh*) Ah well, now what was it I came in for? Really, my memory's gone from bad to worse. Oh, I remember. I was wondering if you had some sort of a suitcase I could borrow. I've only got one of those old-fashioned

161

trunks, and I'm going down to my married sister's for a few days. I thought the change might take my mind off things.

MRS MOFFAT: Yes, I think I can help ye. You wouldn't be wanting to take the case straight away, I suppose?

MRS WESTON: Oh no, there's no great hurry.

MRS MOFFAT: Then I'll have the boy call round in the morning with it.

MRS WESTON: That would do nicely, Mrs Moffat.

MRS MOFFAT: Is it a long journey ye'll be making?

MRS WESTON: Yes, it's a tidy way. Hove. It's near Brighton, ye know. Have ye ever been to Hove?

MRS MOFFAT: No. I'm afraid I haven't. There aren't many places I have been to, Mrs Weston, and that's the truth. I've often thought I'd like to travel, though – providing, of course, I had the time and money. (*A pause*) Now what was it Shakespeare said about travellers?

A pause.

MRS WESTON: (*Seriously*) He said: Travellers ne'er did lie, though fools at home condemn 'em!

MRS MOFFAT gasps.

The door behind her is thrown open.

TEMPLE: Drop that bag, Mrs Weston!

MRS MOFFAT: But, but – surely …

TEMPLE: Come on, Forbes, what are you waiting for?

FORBES: But, Temple, you can't mean that Mrs Weston …

TEMPLE: Sir Graham, allow me to introduce you to the leader of the greatest espionage organisation in Europe – Z.4.

FADE SCENE.
FADE IN dramatic incidental music.

FADE music.
FADE IN STEVE speaking.

STEVE: Another cup of coffee, Sir Graham?

FORBES: No thanks, Steve.

STEVE: (*Pondering*) Darling, there's just one more thing which I don't understand in this whole business and that's I don't see how the devil you account for –

TEMPLE: How the devil I account for the flask?

STEVE: Well, after all, the flask was yours, and there certainly –

TEMPLE: There was certainly cyanide in the flask. Yes, I agree. Still, when Mrs Weston filled that flask for me I don't suppose she intended that Ben should –

STEVE: Oh, Paul, you don't mean she –

TEMPLE: Yes. That was certainly a lucky escape, Steve, as far as I was concerned.

FORBES: At the time it made me more certain than ever that Steiner was Z.4. You see, it was Steiner who suggested the drink in the first place.

TEMPLE: Yes, but Steiner couldn't possibly have known what was in the flask.

FORBES: He might have known, Temple. It's very difficult to say. Incidentally, was the flask your first indication that Mrs Weston was implicated?

163

TEMPLE: No, the flask merely confirmed what was
            already in my mind. I had a pretty shrewd
            suspicion that Mrs Weston had some
            connection with the affair, even at the very
            beginning.

STEVE: But, darling, why?

TEMPLE: Well, in the first place, Ernie Weston returned
            the letter which he had stolen, and which was
            obviously of supreme importance to Z.4.
            Shortly after he returned the letter, Weston was
            murdered. Why? Obviously because he had
            unwittingly let the cat out of the bag about the
            letter.

FORBES: You mean that he had told his wife about it,
            without realising that she was Z.4?

TEMPLE: Exactly. Although, of course, it wasn't quite so
            simple as that at the time. I knew that he'd told
            someone about the letter, and I was pretty sure
            that that someone was Z.4. But it might have
            been Steiner, or possibly Bryant, or possibly
            some other person we had never even heard of.

FORBES: But if it was Bryant or Steiner, then Weston
            must have been on friendly terms with them.

TEMPLE: That point struck me at once. They must, in
            fact, have been well aware that Ernie Weston
            was what is euphemistically termed a
            kleptomaniac. They must have known, in fact,
            that he was in the habit of helping himself to
            other people's possessions. Yet both Bryant
            and Steiner had been obviously puzzled by the
            loss of a watch chain and a pair of cufflinks.

FORBES: Go on …

TEMPLE: Now, assuming that Steiner and Bryant were all
            that they seemed to be, or at any rate were not

definitely connected with Z.4, then obviously Weston must have spoken to someone else – someone, in fact, who knew exactly the sort of game he was playing. It seemed to me that that someone might very easily be an obvious sort of person after all. A person who Weston really would talk to, without attaching any particular importance to it. Someone, in fact, like his wife …

FORBES: Don't try re-lighting that cigar again, Temple. Here, take another.

TEMPLE laughs.

FORBES: The cigars were a present from Rex Bryant. Sort of a quid pro quo in return for an exclusive story.

TEMPLE: Thank you.

TEMPLE lights his new cigar.

FORBES: Well, go on, Temple, let's hear how you narrowed down the field.

TEMPLE: Later, when Steve and I made arrangements to go to Aberdeen and that dreadful accident happened, it became quite obvious that Z.4 was actually at the inn. Only someone staying at the inn could possibly have discovered our arrangements. If any doubt existed in my mind, it was very soon eliminated after our experience at Skerry Lodge.

STEVE: (*Shuddering*) Don't remind me, darling!

FORBES: Yes, but that didn't eliminate Dr Steiner or Rex Bryant as possible suspects. Or Iris Archer, too, for that matter. Remember, all three of them were staying at The Royal Gate.

TEMPLE: If Dr Steiner had been Z.4 it's hardly likely that he'd have interrupted Iris in her search for the letter. Don't forget that she was following instructions received from Z.4.

FORBES: You mean through Mrs Moffat? Yes, that's true.

TEMPLE: Candidly, Sir Graham, I never suspected Rex Bryant from the very first. Finding the watch chain on Weston had quite the opposite effect on me from that intended. It more than convinced me of his innocence.

FORBES: Yes. I rather suspected it was a pretty obvious sort of "plant".

TEMPLE: And now we come to Mrs Weston. Well, in the first place, she was always at the inn, and therefore in a position to overhear most of our conversations; indeed, on one occasion, when we were talking about Lindsay's letter, she actually marched into the room on the pretence of clearing away the coffee things.

FORBES: That seemed natural enough to me at the time.

TEMPLE: Yes, she was a clever little woman, and she had an instinct for time and place. Also, as I have already pointed out, she was the most likely person for her husband to confide in about the letter. And thirdly, she made a very bad slip.

FORBES: (*Shocked*) What do you mean, Temple?

TEMPLE: You probably remember that I discovered certain interesting details about Iris's past. Details which Z.4 knew about, but that Iris was anxious to conceal?

FORBES: Yes.

TEMPLE: I received a telegram which confirmed my suspicions about Iris, but when I received the telegram it had already been opened.

FORBES: You mean Mrs Weston actually opened it herself?

TEMPLE: Precisely. But by mentioning the fact herself, delivering the telegram at a crucial moment, and appearing apparently indifferent to the whole business, the point might very easily have been overlooked. (*He laughs*) I told you she had a nice sense of time and place, Sir Graham.

FORBES: I'm beginning to see daylight. As soon as Mrs Weston read the telegram, she knew that you knew all there was to know about Iris, and that sooner or later Iris would talk.

TEMPLE: Of course you've guessed the secret, Sir Graham?

FORBES takes a letter from his pocket.

FORBES: Yes, yes. This confirms your theory about Mrs Weston. She was definitely the chambermaid at the Martinez Hotel. Even in those days the French authorities suspected her of espionage.

TEMPLE: (*Grinning*) You didn't lose much time checking up, did you, Sir Graham?

STEVE: Paul, you remember when you asked Ernie Weston about your cigarette lighter?

TEMPLE: Yes.

STEVE: What was the idea?

TEMPLE: Oh, that was only to get his reactions, dear. I knew then for a certainly that he was in the habit of helping himself to other people's things, and that in all probability he had been responsible for the letter disappearing.

STEVE: Have the War Office people returned to London yet, Sir Graham?

167

FORBES: Oh yes. There wasn't much they could do at the chalet. The fire totally ruined it. They went through the remains, of course, in the hope that they might find something of Hardwick's plans but it was no use.

STEVE: That poor man ... fancy setting fire to the chalet knowing he'd be killed himself.

FORBES: It's all very sad. What the man was thinking at the end ... well, it's beyond me. (*A pause*) Well, I must be off. But don't forget you're dining with us next Thursday, my wife is counting on it.

TEMPLE: (*Laughing*) Steve is already talking about us taking another holiday, Sir Graham.

FORBES: (*Amused*) Well, you've certainly earned a good rest. Goodbye, Steve.

STEVE: Goodbye, Sir Graham. See you on Thursday.

FORBES: No need to see me out, Temple. I know my way.

TEMPLE: Goodbye, Sir Graham.

The door closes.

TEMPLE: All right, Steve?

STEVE: Yes. It's so lovely to be home again, isn't it?

TEMPLE: (*Laughing*) Does that mean we can stay here for a couple of weeks before you want us to go off on our travels again?

STEVE: Well ... As a matter if fact I was thinking about Lake Como. After all, darling, we haven't been there since our honeymoon.

TEMPLE: Yes.

STEVE: Do you remember that Lake, Paul? It was so blue ... so deep ... and so romantically blue.

TEMPLE: All those lakes were blue, darling.

STEVE: No, that lake at the foot of the forest, that was the bluest of all. You know that lake, I mean the one where we had an argument about fish being able to talk?

TEMPLE: Which argument?

STEVE: (*Wistfully*) Our first one …

TEMPLE: (*Laughing*) Oh yes! It was a hell of a row for honeymooners! What a start to our married life!

FADE IN closing music.

THE END

Press Pack
Press cuttings about News of Paul Temple …

News of Paul Temple
Martyn C. Webster, who produced all the Paul Temple radio serials, describes how Paul Temple came into being.

The name Paul Temple is now familiar to thousands of listeners in the British Isles, Australia, New Zealand, and Holland, where the radio serials have been broadcast. I can remember that afternoon so well, when Francis Durbridge and I were racking our brains to think of a new show that would get listeners. Every idea we had seemed to have been done before and we were getting rather desperate. Then one of us – I can't remember which – had a brainwave. We phoned several libraries and bookshops and asked them what kind of book was mostly in demand, and without exception their reply was "Detective novels and thrillers".

That settled it. If that was the popular demand, then it was up to us to do something about it. So Francis Durbridge went home to burn the midnight oil. He returned a week later with a synopsis of the first episode of a serial thriller – or rather, as he stipulated, a serial play, which was to be presented in eight weekly instalments of twenty-five minutes each. He said he wanted to intrigue listeners rather than thrill them. And he certainly did intrigue me by his synopsis.

One thing was missing, however – the name of the new radio sleuth. Francis had a long list of possible names, but somehow they didn't sound right, or were reminiscent of The Saint or Lord Peter Wimsey. So we left it for the time being.

A few nights later the phone rang – at one a.m. to be precise. It was Francis Durbridge. "What do you feel about

Paul Temple for the name of our friend?" he asked. Excellent. So Paul Temple came into being.

Then came the problem of casting. After a fortnight we had a cast list complete, with the exception of the two principals: Paul Temple and Steve. In Temple we had to have someone with microphone experience together with a dominant personality, and yet the lightness so essential for the character. We tried about fourteen actors and finally decided upon that versatile young man Hugh Morton. We had the same problem with Steve. She had to have a soft, warm voice, and yet be capable of rising to emotional heights. We tried several people without success, and then one day, I listened to a Children's Hour play, and the girl who played the leading part was just our idea of Steve. Her name was Bernadette Hodgson, and it was gratifying to find that her appearance was in keeping with her voice. Not that that really matters to a radio producer, but, as I said, it was gratifying!

I don't think I have ever enjoyed producing a show so much. I had an excellent script, a helpful and congenial author, and a grand cast to work with, and if ever there was a team spirit we had it in that production.

To sustain their interest I only gave the members of the cast the script of each episode as we did it. Consequently they had no idea at all who the Knave of Diamonds was. And it was quite stimulating for Francis Durbridge and me to watch their reactions during the first reading of each episode. They had a sweepstake on which of them was the Knave and not until the first rehearsal of the last episode was their curiosity satisfied.

Yes, we enjoyed our Paul Temple. And so, I think, did many listeners, as after our first serial we had 7,500 letters of appreciation.

It's a very pleasant thought for me that I am to do another serial, called *News of Paul Temple*, which begins on November 13. But I shan't tell you anything about it! Except that at least two of the originals – Paul Temple and Steve – will be with you again.

November 13! I've only just realised it! Thank heavens it's not a Friday!

Paul Temple

With all due respect to serial versions of the classics, there is quite a different sort of thrill about a serial in which you cannot anticipate the ending by looking at the back of the book. No broadcast serials have been made more successful than the Paul Temple stories, and we are glad to know that the latest adventure of Paul Temple, written by Francis Durbridge, is to be broadcast from November 13 onwards, every Monday at 6.15. Hugh Morton will again take the name part, with Bernadette Hodgson again as his inseparable Steve. Martyn Webster will produce.

This time the impeccable Paul, with his attractive wife, is coming back from America (by air) to work on the production of his new play. Iris Archer, the famous actress, is to play the lead, but suddenly and unaccountably she throws up the part. Paul and Steve go to Scotland on holiday and at once get mixed up in a most sinister affair of espionage, with doped cigarettes, shootings, mysterious inventions, and a super-spy whom nobody has ever seen, known only as Z.4. From what we have heard about this serial, you will be on tenterhooks from the beginning to the end.

RETURN OF PAUL TEMPLE!

Paul Temple and his wife Steve land in England from the transatlantic 'Golden Clipper', and arrive to find themselves soon mixed up in an adventure even more enthralling than that of *The Front Page Men*. This evening at 6.15 a new weekly serial play *News of Paul Temple* begins.

'*Haven't much time . . . wallet . . . where on earth did . . . driving licence . . . insurance certificate . . .*'

Iris Archer feverishly searches Paul Temple's pockets for the mysterious letter addressed to John Richmond. The second episode of *News of Paul Temple* will be broadcast this evening at 6.15.

'*Paul Temple and wife motoring to Aberdeen tomorrow morning . . . Imperative that they do not reach there . . . Z4.*'

The mysterious Z4 shows his true colours in the third episode of *News of Paul Temple*, to be broadcast this evening at 6.15.

'News of Paul Temple'. In the fourth episode this evening at 6.15 Paul Temple and Steve have a watery welcome when they visit the inventor of the Hardwick Screen at Skerry Lodge!

WHO IS Z4? Iris Archer says 'No one knows the identity of Z4 . . . not even the impeccable Paul Temple'. But is she right? The fifth thrilling episode of *News of Paul Temple* will be broadcast this evening at 6.15. This is the listener's last chance to solve the mystery of Z4 for himself before the story finishes next week.

**Paul Vlaanderen
en het Z-4 Mysterie**

Een detectivespel van Francis Durbridge

.25 EEN AFSPRAAK MET HET GEVAAR **10.10**

Paul Vlaanderen en het Z-4 Mysterie
EEN DETECTIVE HOORSPEL
VAN FRANCIS DURBRIDGE
● ● ●
Tweede episode: Betreft Z-4

9.35   10.10

www.ingramcontent.com/pod-product-compliance
Lightning Source LLC
Chambersburg PA
CBHW020845260626
47169CB00003B/1140